CLOTHED BY LOVE

CYNTHIA CHIRINDA

Wholeness
Incorporated
Publishing

Clothed By Love
By Cynthia Chirinda

CONTENTS

CLOTHED
BY LOVE

CHAPTER ONE

WHISPERS

OF LIGHT

T he dawn arrived gently over Nyathera, washing the village in hues of gold and amber. The sun stretched its fingers across red clay roads, lush green fields, and vibrant market stalls that were slowly coming to life. The scent of fresh bread and wood smoke curled through the air like a warm embrace.

Abeni stepped out of her family's small home, a woven basket filled with freshly pressed linens balanced on her hip. Behind her, Mama Tandiwe sat by the window, stitching bright patterns into a length of fabric. Her hands worked with practiced grace, the needle gliding effortlessly through the material.

"Abeni," Mama Tandiwe called gently, her voice as soothing as warm honey. "Remember, my girl, the way you carry yourself speaks louder than any words you could ever say."

Abeni paused and turned back, her smile soft and sincere. "Yes, Mama. Today will be a good day, I feel it."

With her mother's gentle encouragement lingering in her ears, Abeni started her walk to the expatriate homes. The path led her past neighbors who greeted her with warm smiles, and children who called out her name between fits of laughter.

As she walked through a shaded path lined with ancient trees, the leaves whispered secrets in the breeze, and Abeni whispered back.

"Lord, guide me today. Help me see the beauty in every moment, even the small ones. And help others see You through me."

The path opened up to the whitewashed estate houses that sat at the edge of Nyathera. Their grandeur stood in contrast to the simple beauty of the village, yet Abeni approached them with a quiet strength that carried her forward.

∾· The Sterling Household ·∾

The Sterling estate was surrounded by flowering gardens—roses, lavender, and lilies swaying in the morning breeze. Abeni knocked softly on the back kitchen door, her hands steady despite the flutter of uncertainty in her chest.

The door creaked open, revealing Mrs. Sterling, Lucas' mother. Her expression was warm, though her eyes seemed distracted by distant worries.

"Good morning, Abeni! Come in, dear. The linens for the guest rooms are in the hallway upstairs."

"Good morning, ma'am," Abeni replied softly, stepping inside with her basket balanced neatly on her hip.

As she climbed the grand staircase, the weight of the basket familiar against her hip, Abeni caught sight of Lucas through a large window overlooking the garden. He was sitting beneath an ancient tree, a book resting open in his lap, sunlight catching the golden tones in his wavy hair.

Their eyes met briefly. Lucas' gaze was steady, curious, and unguarded.

"There was something in his gaze—an openness, a quiet curiosity. But he was a world apart from me, wasn't he?"

She looked away quickly, her heart fluttering in her chest, and continued up the stairs.

∾· The Balcony Encounter ·∾

Later in the day, as Abeni shook out a blanket on one of the guest room balconies, she noticed Lucas walking below with a cup of tea in hand. He glanced up, spotting her before she could step back inside.

"Good morning," Lucas said, his voice carrying easily across the space.

Abeni hesitated for a heartbeat before replying softly, "Good morning, sir."

"You don't have to call me 'sir,'" Lucas said lightly. "I'm Lucas."

Abeni's lips pressed into a faint smile, but she said nothing more. The weight of the moment felt fragile, and she feared breaking it with unnecessary words.

Lucas lingered for a moment longer, his eyes filled with something unspoken, before he continued down the garden path.

❧ *Reflections at Sunset* ❧

The sun dipped below the horizon as Abeni made her way home. The sky blazed with hues of pink and gold, the colors melting into one another as if painted by unseen hands.

The walk felt longer that evening, her thoughts lingering on the brief exchange with Lucas.

"It was nothing—a passing exchange. And yet... why does it linger so deeply in my mind?"

When she arrived home, Mama Tandiwe was still seated by the window, her sewing work now illuminated by the flickering light of an oil lamp. She looked up and met her daughter's gaze with a knowing smile.

"Sometimes, child," Mama Tandiwe said softly, "God writes stories in the most unexpected places. You just have to be ready to read them."

Abeni nodded, a small smile tugging at her lips. She set her basket down and sat beside her mother, her hands gently resting on the woven fibers as the lamplight cast soft, golden shadows across the room.

The evening wrapped itself around their home like a warm embrace, leaving Abeni with a quiet sense of peace—and a flicker of something she couldn't yet name.

CHAPTER TWO

LUCAS' WORLD

The sun dipped low over the sprawling Sterling estate, casting long golden shadows across the whitewashed walls and manicured gardens. Birds sang their evening songs as the faint scent of lavender lingered in the warm breeze. Behind the tall iron gates, the world of the Sterlings stood starkly apart from the vibrant rhythms of Nyathera village.

Lucas Alexander Sterling sat on the balcony of his family's study, a worn leather-bound journal open in his lap. His blue-gray eyes scanned the horizon, taking in the distant rooftops of Nyathera, where life carried on in bright colors and unfiltered joy. It was a stark contrast to the polished corridors and pristine orderliness of his family's home.

The Sterling Legacy

Mr. James Sterling, Lucas' father, was a man of structure and ambition. The Sterling family had come to Nyathera nearly five years ago with a vision—to establish a trade route for rare spices and handcrafted textiles. The venture was profitable but grueling, and it had taken a toll on the family. Lucas' mother, Eleanor Sterling, played the role of the dutiful wife with practiced grace, often hosting gatherings and managing the social demands of expatriate life.

At the dinner table, James Sterling spoke with a clipped tone, his brow furrowed as he examined a stack of trade ledgers.

"The local partnerships are too fragile," he muttered. "We need consistency. Loyalty. These small-scale artisans are unpredictable."

Eleanor, seated across the table, glanced at Lucas, her voice soft. "James, perhaps if you approached them differently, if you understood their ways…"

James waved her off. "Understanding won't change numbers, Eleanor."

Lucas pushed his food around on his plate, his appetite fading.

"What do you think, Lucas?" his father asked abruptly. "You've been spending time around the village. What do you see?"

Lucas hesitated. "I see people who work hard, who care deeply about their craft. But they're not driven by profits—they're driven by legacy, by family."

James sighed. "You have a romantic view of the world, son. Business isn't about sentimentality."

Lucas' jaw tightened, but he said nothing.

The Weight of Expectation

That evening, Lucas retreated to the small study tucked away at the far end of the estate. The walls were lined with books—everything from philosophy to economic theories. A half-finished sketch of the Nyathera marketplace lay spread across his desk, charcoal smudges staining his fingers.

His mother entered quietly, her soft footsteps muffled by the thick carpet.

"Lucas," she began, her voice gentle. "Your father… he's hard on you because he sees so much of himself in you. But you're different. You see people, not just numbers."

Lucas looked up, his expression weary. "But he expects me to follow his path, Mother. Build empires, make deals, expand territories. But… I'm not sure that's what I want."

Eleanor sighed, brushing a lock of Lucas' hair back from his forehead. "You have a good heart, Lucas. Follow it. Even if it leads you somewhere unexpected."

Lucas turned back to his sketch, but his mind wandered—to the village, to the vibrant sounds and colors of Nyathera, and to a pair of warm brown eyes he had only just begun to know.

‿ A Stroll Beyond the Gates ·‿

The next morning, Lucas slipped out of the estate under the soft glow of dawn, clutching a leather satchel filled with sketching supplies. He walked down the dusty red clay road that led toward the heart of Nyathera.

The marketplace was beginning to stir—women setting up colorful stalls, children weaving between them with baskets balanced on their heads, and the distant sound of a drum marking the morning's arrival.

Lucas found a shaded corner near a fruit stand and began sketching the scene. His pencil moved quickly across the page, capturing the lively expressions, the vibrant fabrics, and the warmth that seemed to radiate from every interaction.

"Your hands move like they're telling a story," a soft voice said from behind him.

Startled, Lucas turned to find Abeni standing there, her basket balanced on her hip, her head tilted slightly in curiosity.

He smiled sheepishly. "I suppose they are. Every face here has a story worth telling."

Abeni nodded. "And every story deserves to be told with care."

For a moment, silence stretched between them—comfortable, unhurried.

"You're not like the others," Abeni said softly, her gaze steady. "You see things differently."

Lucas swallowed hard, her words settling deep in his chest. "Maybe because I'm still trying to figure out who I am."

He went quiet as he reflected within himself quietly. *"I'm supposed to follow my father into the family business, but I'm not sure it's what I want. I'm still fairly young, and yet it feels like every decision I make is set in stone."*

At twenty-six, Lucas felt as though he carried the weight of choices that would shape a lifetime.

Abeni's lips curved into a faint smile before she turned and walked away, disappearing into the bustling crowd.

Lucas watched her go, a strange feeling stirring in his chest—a mix of admiration, curiosity, and something he couldn't yet name.

∽· Seeds of Change ·∽

Back at the estate, Lucas sat by the window in his room, staring out at the distant village.

His father's voice echoed in his mind: *"Business isn't about sentimentality."*

But Lucas couldn't stop thinking about Nyathera—the people, the stories, and Abeni. He felt drawn to the village not just out of curiosity but out of something deeper—a desire to understand, to connect, and perhaps… to belong.

Pulling out his journal, he scribbled a single sentence:

"Sometimes, the heart knows long before the mind catches up."

In the quiet spaces between duty and desire, Lucas began
to glimpse the life he longed to live—a life stitched together not
by expectations, but by love and purpose.

CHAPTER Three

SEEDS OF FRIENDSHIP

The golden light of morning poured through the cracks of Nyathera's sky. The sun stretched across the horizon as the village stirred awake. Roosters crowed in the distance, and the faint chatter of morning voices mingled with the rhythmic clinking of metal pots. Abeni walked briskly along the familiar path toward the Sterling estate, her woven basket balanced gracefully on her hip. The sky, painted in hues of orange and soft pink, seemed to whisper promises of hope.

She paused briefly by the riverbank, where the water glistened like scattered jewels under the rising sun. A soft breeze rustled the reeds along the shore. Kneeling by the edge, she dipped her fingers into the cool water and whispered a quiet prayer:

"Lord, guide my hands and my heart today. Let me see Your love in every moment, and let others see You in me."

A soft breeze brushed against her cheek as if carrying an unseen answer. A bird sang overhead, as if in response. Abeni smiled softly, her heart steadied by the familiar rhythm of faith. Adjusting her basket, she rose and continued her journey.

✑· *An Unplanned Conversation* ·✑

At the Sterling estate, the house felt unusually quiet. Mrs. Sterling had left early for a community meeting, and the silence hung like a fragile thread in the grand house. In the kitchen, Abeni sliced fruit for breakfast, her movements swift and deliberate. The sun filtered through the sheer curtains, casting delicate patterns on the kitchen tiles as Abeni carefully sliced fruit for breakfast. The scent of ripe mangoes and freshly brewed tea filled the air.

She didn't hear Lucas enter until his voice broke the silence.

"Good morning, Abeni."

The voice startled her slightly, and she turned to see Lucas leaning casually against the kitchen doorway. His hair caught the light, and his blue eyes carried a thoughtful expression.

Her hand paused mid-slice, and she looked up, her eyes briefly wide with surprise.

"Good morning, Lucas," Abeni replied, her eyes returning quickly to her task.

He leaned casually against the doorframe, arms crossed, a faint smile playing on his lips.

Lucas hesitated before stepping closer, his hands tucked into his pockets.

"You always look so focused. Like you're carrying something heavy, even when you're doing something as simple as slicing fruit."

Abeni's brow furrowed slightly as she considered his words. She paused, the knife still in her hand, and looked up, her gaze steady.

"Sometimes, Lucas, when you're given much to carry, you learn not to stumble."

Her words, simple yet profound, seemed to catch Lucas off guard. He leaned back slightly.

"Do you ever slow down, Abeni? Take a moment for yourself?"

Abeni tilted her head, her lips curving into a faint smile. *"In moments like this. When the world is quiet, and someone asks a question worth answering."*

The weight of her words seemed to settle between them. Lucas' smile softened, and he nodded slowly, as though understanding something unspoken.

For a moment, neither spoke. The stillness wrapped around them like a fragile cocoon before Abeni returned to slicing fruit.

Before Lucas could respond, a distant bell rang, signaling an arrival at the estate's front gate. He straightened, offered her one more lingering glance, and walked away.

Abeni exhaled slowly, realizing she had been holding her breath.

At twenty-three, the weight of responsibility often felt heavier than the basket she carried on her hip. But here, in this moment, Lucas' questions made her feel… seen.

Abeni carried herself with a grace and wisdom that often made others forget her youth.

"Why does his kindness feel so heavy, yet so light all at once?"

ℯ∾∙ An Exchange in the Garden ∙∾℮

The afternoon sun hung lower in the sky as Abeni worked in the Sterling garden, her hands buried in soft earth as she planted herbs. The scents of rosemary and lavender filled the air, mingling with the faint sound of birdsong.

Lucas appeared from around the corner, holding a small, weathered book.

"Do you like stories, Abeni?" he asked.

Abeni paused, wiping her hands on her apron. "Stories are the threads of life, Lucas. They weave meaning into the quietest moments."

Lucas crouched beside her, offering her the book. Its leather cover was worn, and the corners were frayed with age.

"This belonged to my grandmother," Lucas explained softly. *"She loved poetry. I think you'd like it."*

Abeni hesitated, her hands still dusted with earth, before gently taking the book. She brushed her fingertips over the worn cover as though it were something sacred.

"Thank you, Lucas. But why share something so precious with me?"

Lucas's eyes softened.

"Because stories deserve to be shared with people who understand their value."

His voice was quiet, but his words carried weight. For a brief moment, their eyes met, and the unspoken connection between them deepened.

"Thank you, Lucas. I'll take care of it."

Lucas smiled faintly before rising to his feet and walking back toward the house.

There was something in his smile—something warm, genuine, and disarming—that made Abeni's heart flutter in a way she didn't quite understand.

Abeni clutched the book to her chest, her heart filled with gratitude and something else—a feeling she couldn't yet name.

The sun had dipped low by the time Abeni returned home. The poetry book rested safely in her basket, tucked beneath a folded scarf.

✑ Mama Tandiwe's Wisdom ✑

That evening, Abeni sat cross-legged on the floor of their small home, the poetry book resting on her lap. The fire crackled softly in the background, casting flickering shadows on the walls.

Mama Tandiwe glanced up from her sewing and raised an eyebrow.

"That's not one of your usual books, my child."

Abeni's fingers traced the edge of the leather cover. "It's a gift, Mama. From Lucas."

Mama Tandiwe set her needle aside and studied her daughter carefully.

"This boy… he sees something in you, Abeni."

Abeni's gaze dropped to the book. "Mama, his world is so different from ours. How could anything real grow from this?"

Mama Tandiwe's voice softened. "My girl, the soil doesn't ask where a seed comes from. It simply gives it a place to grow."

Abeni's eyes glistened with tears as she nodded, her mother's words settling deep in her spirit.

That night, Abeni sat outside their home, the sky spread above her like an endless tapestry. The poetry book lay open on her lap, its pages illuminated by the faint glow of the moon.

She read aloud softly:

"'Love knows no boundaries, no borders, no walls. It speaks in whispers and waits patiently to be heard.'"

Her voice caught on the final word, and she pressed the book gently against her chest.

"Lord, if this is part of Your plan, guide me. If it's not, guard me."

The wind whispered softly through the trees, carrying her prayer into the night.

CHAPTER Four

ROOTS OF FAITH

The dawn light spilled gently over the humble clay walls of Mama Tandiwe's home. Inside, the smell of warm porridge and herbal tea filled the air. Abeni, no older than eight, sat cross-legged on a woven mat near her father, Baba Luthando, who was mending a broken fishing net. His hands moved with careful precision, his brow furrowed in focus.

"Abeni," he said, his deep voice gentle yet firm, "every knot in this net serves a purpose. Miss one, and the fish will slip away."

Young Abeni nodded, her dark eyes wide with understanding. "Like how every prayer matters, Baba?"

He smiled faintly, his weathered face softening. "Yes, my child. Every prayer is like a knot—a connection between us and God."

Mama Tandiwe entered, carrying a small basket of fresh bread. Her eyes, sharp but warm, took in the scene. "Luthando, you'll fill our daughter's head with too many thoughts before she's had her breakfast."

Laughter danced between them, and for a fleeting moment, their small home felt like the safest place in the world.

✎∙ Lessons by the River ∙✎

Abeni followed her father down to the riverbank later that day. The water glittered in the midday sun, and a cool breeze stirred the reeds. Baba Luthando knelt by the river, his reflection rippling in the water.

"Do you know why we pray by the river, Abeni?" he asked.

She shook her head.

"Because the river listens. It carries our prayers to places we cannot reach ourselves."

He placed a smooth stone in her hand. "This stone, child, has been shaped by water over time—softened, refined. Life will shape you the same way if you let God guide the current."

Abeni clutched the stone tightly, her young mind absorbing every word.

✑· A Day Remembered ·✑

After their time at the river, Abeni and her father walked back home together, the smooth stone nestled safely in her palm. The midday sun filtered gently through the trees, and Baba Luthando's voice carried softly as he pointed out the flight of birds or paused to greet a neighbor. He seemed lighter that day—thoughtful, but at peace.

When they arrived home, Mama Tandiwe had just finished setting out lunch beneath the shade of the jacaranda tree. A pot of sadza steamed beside a dish of dried fish and pumpkin leaves.

"You two took your time," Mama Tandiwe said with a teasing smile.

"Your husband made me a philosopher today," Abeni grinned, slipping onto the reed mat. "He said the river listens."

Baba Luthando chuckled as he sat beside them. "And she listened well."

The small family shared their meal with quiet joy—passing the bowls, trading gentle jokes, and savoring the ordinary sacredness of being together.

After lunch, Baba Luthando rose and kissed the top of Abeni's head. "The waters will not wait," he said. "I'll check the nets before dusk."

Mama Tandiwe handed him a wrapped parcel of dried bread and a calabash of water. "Don't stay too long, Luthando. The wind smells like change."

He nodded solemnly, and with one final glance at his wife and daughter, he turned down the familiar path toward the river.

Abeni spent the rest of the afternoon helping her mother sweep the yard and rinse the linens. Later, she ran off to join her friends beneath the neem tree near the well. They played clapping games, told silly stories, and sang call-and-response songs until their laughter echoed through the village like birds in flight.

As dusk approached, Abeni skipped home, barefoot and carefree, her heart still light from the joy of the day. The stone her father had given her remained in her pocket, warm and steady.

She didn't know it then, but it would be the last day she would ever see her father.

ಎം· Loss and Shadows ·ಎං

The golden hues of dusk cast long shadows over the village as Abeni sat by the doorway, waiting for her father to return from fishing. Mama Tandiwe sat nearby, her sewing basket resting at her feet.

But Baba Luthando never returned that night.

Days later, his empty fishing boat was found drifting downstream, tangled in reeds and half-filled with water. The villagers gathered in hushed tones, offering condolences and murmured prayers.

Abeni stood by her mother's side, clutching the stone her father had given her. The world felt colder, heavier.

Mama Tandiwe's voice broke through the fog of grief. "We must trust God, Abeni. Even in this darkness, He is still the light."

Abeni nodded, her young face streaked with silent tears.

ಎం· Whispers of Resilience ·ಎং

Life changed after Baba Luthando's passing. Mama Tandiwe took on more sewing work, her fingers moving tirelessly over fabric late into the night.

Abeni learned to carry burdens far larger than her small shoulders. She helped her mother with chores, delivered fabric to neighbors, and spent long hours at the market selling homemade crafts.

But in the quiet moments—when the village was still and the stars shimmered above—Abeni would slip away to the riverbank. She would kneel by the water, clutch the smooth stone her father had given her, and whisper prayers into the night.

"Lord, guide me like You guided Baba. Keep Mama safe. And please... let me grow strong like this stone."

The river always seemed to answer, its gentle murmurs carrying her words into the unknown.

The Burden of Whispers

As Abeni grew older, the whispers in the village began. Some villagers spoke kindly of her family, admiring Mama Tandiwe's strength and Abeni's diligence. Others, however, were less kind.

"That girl carries too much weight on her shoulders," an old woman muttered one day at the market.

"Without a father's guidance, she'll lose her way," another chimed in.

Abeni overheard the words but said nothing. She had learned to let such comments slide off her like water over river stones.

But deep down, they stung.

One evening, as she sat with Mama Tandiwe sewing under the soft glow of an oil lamp, Abeni spoke softly. "Mama, do you think Baba can still hear us?"

Mama Tandiwe looked up, her eyes glistening. "Yes, my child. And more importantly, God hears us too. He sees every tear, every stitch, every prayer."

Abeni nodded and resumed sewing, her hands steady, her heart anchored in faith.

It was during one of these long sewing nights that Abeni began to dream.

"Mama," she said one evening, her voice hesitant but determined. "What if we could teach other girls to sew? What if we could create something... something bigger than just these dresses?"

Mama Tandiwe looked at her daughter with quiet pride. "Dreams, my child, are seeds. Plant them in faith, water them with hard work, and watch them grow."

From that night onward, every stitch Abeni sewed carried with it a prayer, a hope, and a seed of her dream.

In the threads of loss and the stitches of faith,
Abeni's story began to weave itself into
something greater—something eternal.

CHAPTER *FIVE*:

WHISPERS IN THE WIND

The day had begun with a stillness that carried an air of expectancy. The sky hung heavy with clouds, and the sun seemed reluctant to break through their veil. Nyathera's marketplace bustled with hurried footsteps and anxious voices as villagers prepared for the coming storm.

At the Sterling estate, the air felt equally heavy—not with rain, but with something unspoken.

❧• An Invitation Unfolds •❧

Abeni arrived earlier than usual, her steps quick and deliberate. She adjusted the basket on her hip and inhaled deeply as she walked through the iron gates. The garden was alive with movement—workers arranging flowers, setting tables, and carrying trays laden with crystal glasses.

Mrs. Sterling spotted her and approached with a warm smile.

"Abeni, dear, we're hosting guests this evening. Would you be able to stay a little longer to help us?"

Abeni hesitated. Staying beyond her usual hours felt unfamiliar, but Mrs. Sterling's gentle smile made it difficult to refuse.

"Yes, ma'am. I'll stay."

From across the courtyard, Lucas stood by a window, his gaze lingering on Abeni as she disappeared into the house. His smile was small, but his eyes were bright with something he couldn't quite name.

ᏜᎶ A Quiet Garden Moment ᏜᎶ

The afternoon sun painted dappled shadows on the garden path as Abeni arranged freshly laundered linens on a wooden line. Lucas approached, hands tucked into his pockets, his brow furrowed with thought.

"Abeni," he said softly, his voice threading through the quiet air.

She turned, basket in hand, her smile faltering at the look in his eyes. "Lucas... is something wrong?"

He hesitated, his gaze flickering towards the horizon before settling back on her. "My father... he's been talking about leaving Nyathera. The business isn't doing well, and he thinks it's time to return to Europe."

Abeni's breath caught in her throat. The distant chatter of birds and the rustling leaves seemed to amplify the silence between them.

"When?" she asked quietly.

"I don't know. Soon, maybe. Nothing is decided yet, but... it feels final somehow."

Abeni looked down at her hands, gripping the basket tighter. "Nyathera will feel different without you, Lucas."

Lucas stepped closer, his voice low. "I don't want to leave. Not like this. Not... without you knowing how much this place—how much you—mean to me."

Abeni looked up, her eyes glistening with unshed tears. But before she could respond, the distant voice of Mrs. Sterling called Lucas back into the house.

He hesitated, his eyes lingering on her face for one final moment before turning and walking away.

Abeni was left to her quiet thoughts.

"Some moments feel heavy, as if they carry the weight of everything unsaid. And yet, they pass—silent, fragile, but unforgettable."

❧• *A Moment of Honesty* •❧

The evening descended with the slow hush of twilight. Lanterns hung from branches, casting golden halos onto the garden paths. Guests began to arrive in clusters, their laughter and conversation weaving together into a soft hum.

Abeni moved gracefully between tables, balancing a tray of refreshments. She stayed in the shadows, her presence quiet yet indispensable.

Near a lantern-lit corner, Lucas found her. He stepped closer, his crisp white shirt glowing faintly in the lantern light.

"You stayed," he said softly, his voice almost lost in the distant hum of the party.

Abeni paused, her eyes lifting to meet his. "Your mother asked me to."

"I'm glad," Lucas replied, his voice carrying a sincerity that made Abeni's chest tighten slightly. "It's... nice seeing you here, like this."

For a brief moment, the world around them dimmed—the distant laughter, the tinkling glasses, the flickering lantern light—all faded away.

"Do you ever dream, Abeni?" Lucas asked suddenly.

Abeni hesitated, her fingers brushing against the tray's edge. "Dreams are stitched into every dress I sew, Lucas. They live in the folds of the fabric, in every careful thread."

Lucas' gaze softened, and he took a small step closer. "That's beautiful."

But before either of them could say more, a voice called Lucas' name from across the garden. He hesitated, holding her gaze for one final lingering moment before walking away.

Abeni let out a breath she hadn't realized she was holding.

"Lord, why does my heart feel so unsteady around him?"

❧• *A Gift Shared* •❧

The evening wound down, and the lantern light began to flicker as the night deepened. The guests slowly drifted away, their laughter fading into the cool night air.

Abeni stood near the veranda, folding table linens with practiced precision. The quiet felt heavy, almost sacred.

Lucas appeared again, stepping onto the veranda with a small box in his hand, wrapped in brown paper.

"I wanted to give you something," he said, holding it out to her.

Abeni hesitated before accepting it, her fingers trembling slightly as she undid the string. Inside lay a delicate silver cross pendant resting on a piece of velvet cloth.

"It belonged to my grandmother," Lucas said softly. "She always said love should be worn close to the heart."

Abeni's throat tightened, and her voice was barely above a whisper. "Lucas, I... I cannot accept this."

"Please," Lucas said, his voice steady yet gentle. "It's not just a gift. It's... a promise. A reminder that someone sees you—not just the work you do, but who you are."

Their eyes met—unspoken words passing between them like threads pulled tight. Lucas stepped forward slowly, asking with his eyes before reaching behind her neck.

"May I?"

Abeni gave a small nod.

His fingers brushed against her skin as he clasped the chain gently in place. The pendant settled just above her heart, its silver surface catching the lantern light.

She looked down at it, her fingers resting over the cross.

"Thank you, Lucas," she whispered. "I'll treasure it."

In that brief, sacred moment, something shifted—something unspoken yet undeniably real. A thread stitched quietly into the fabric of their story.

❧· Mama Tandiwe's Wisdom ·❧

Later that night, Abeni sat cross-legged on the floor of their small home, the pendant gleaming faintly against her skin. The fire crackled in the corner, casting soft shadows across the room.

She reached up and gently touched the cross, her fingers tracing its delicate edges.

Mama Tandiwe glanced up from her sewing, her eyes immediately catching the glint of silver. She set her needle down.

"Child, your eyes are carrying questions tonight. And that pendant… it carries a story."

Abeni's voice was soft, uncertain. "Mama, Lucas gave it to me. He said it was his grandmother's. He placed it on me… and it feels heavy. Not just here." She touched her chest. "But here too." Her voice trembled as she placed her hand over her heart.

Mama Tandiwe leaned closer, her voice a blend of tenderness and truth.

"Love, real love, my child, is both heavy and light. It carries the weight of truth, but it also lifts the soul. Do not fear it, Abeni. If God has placed it in your path, He will guide you through it."

Abeni nodded, her eyes glistening. Mama Tandiwe reached over and cupped her daughter's face in her hands.

"Trust His timing, Abeni. Trust His story."

The pendant rested quietly against her heart—no longer just a gift, but a beginning.

❧· A Whisper in the Night ·❧

Under the wide canopy of stars, Abeni stood outside their home. The pendant hung around her neck, catching the faint moonlight.

She clutched it gently and whispered into the night:

"Lord, if love is truly part of Your plan, let it grow as You will. If not, let me have the strength to let it go."

The night wind stirred the leaves, carrying her prayer away into the vast darkness. Somewhere in the distance, the river murmured faintly—soft and steady, like the voice of God reminding her: *the current still carries your story.*

CHAPTER *SIX*

THE GROWING STORM

T he skies over Nyathera carried the weight of gathering clouds, their gray bellies heavy with impending rain. The usual vibrancy of the village market was subdued, with merchants packing their goods under hastily tied tarpaulins.

Abeni moved through the narrow paths with her basket balanced on her hip, her face calm but her mind a tangle of thoughts. Ever since Lucas had shared his family's plans to leave Nyathera, a shadow had been cast over her days.

Mama Tandiwe had noticed the faraway look in her daughter's eyes.

"The skies reflect your heart today, Abeni," she said softly one morning as she stitched a hem.

Abeni glanced up, her lips pressed into a faint smile. "It feels like something is slipping away, Mama. Like sand through my fingers."

Mama Tandiwe reached over and squeezed her daughter's hand.

"Sometimes, child, God allows storms to clear paths we cannot see. Trust Him."

✎• The Sterling Family Fractures •✎

At the Sterling estate, the tension was palpable. Mr. Sterling paced in his study, a letter from his business partners in Europe clutched tightly in his hand. The family had been in Nyathera for almost five years, overseeing agricultural exports—coffee beans, cocoa, and rare herbs. But the business was struggling; supply lines were inconsistent, and European demand was waning.

Mrs. Sterling sat by the window, her face drawn with quiet worry. She had always been the softer presence in the Sterling household, a bridge between her husband's rigid pragmatism and Lucas' tender heart.

"James," she said gently, "Lucas loves it here. Nyathera has become his home."

Mr. Sterling turned sharply. "Home? This is not our home, Eleanor. This was a chapter—an investment gone sour. We must cut our losses and return to stability."

"And Lucas?" she asked quietly.

"He'll adjust. He's young. He'll forget."

But Mr. Sterling underestimated the depth of his son's roots in Nyathera—and in Abeni.

✐· Lucas' Quiet Realization

That evening, Lucas sat alone in the study, the room dimly lit by the amber glow of a lantern. Before him lay an open journal, its pages filled with half-finished sketches and scribbled thoughts.

He dipped his pen in ink, hesitating before writing.

Abeni.

He stared at the name for a long moment before continuing.

Why does your voice still echo when the garden falls silent? Why do I feel peace just watching you stitch sunlight into fabric?

He paused, then wrote slower this time:

It cannot be just admiration. Not when my heart beats like this.

He closed the journal, his fingers lingering on the cover. He wasn't ready to say the word aloud yet—but in the quiet, he knew.

✐· Whispers in the Market ·✐

The whispers in the village had grown louder. Abeni felt their weight every time she walked through the market square.

"Did you see her speaking with the Sterling boy again?"

"Those worlds don't mix. It's foolishness."

"She'll only end up hurt."

Abeni kept her head held high, her steps steady, but the sting of their words lingered. It wasn't just about her and Lucas—it was about the walls built by generations, the unspoken rules etched into the fabric of both their worlds.

One afternoon, as Abeni was leaving the market, Elder Jabari approached her. His wise eyes studied her carefully.

"Abeni, child," he said gently, "do not let the voices of others drown out the whispers of your heart. But also... tread carefully. Not every bridge is sturdy enough to hold the weight of two worlds."

Abeni nodded, her chest tightening.

❧· A Moment in the Garden ·❧

The next afternoon, Abeni was in the garden again, gently separating flower petals into small bowls. Her fingers moved with habitual grace, but her thoughts wandered.

Lucas approached, his steps deliberate yet soft. He paused, watching her work for a moment.

"Do you ever wonder," he said quietly, "why some people feel like home even if you've only just begun to know them?"

Abeni's hands stilled.

Her gaze remained on the petals, but a faint blush crept up her cheeks. She lowered her eyes, suddenly aware of the warmth in her chest.

"Yes," she replied, her voice hushed. "Sometimes it's the spirit that remembers before the mind understands."

Lucas smiled faintly. "If things were different... I would ask to stay."

She didn't look at him, but her fingers began to twirl the edge of a rose petal between them—delicate, intentional, betraying her stillness.

"And if you asked?" she asked, her voice barely audible.

He stepped closer, his voice no longer tentative. "Then I'd be asking not just to stay—but to build something here. With you."

Abeni turned slightly, her eyes darting to the garden path. Her hands moved to straighten her headwrap—a familiar gesture, though her wrap needed no fixing.

She said nothing.

But the silence trembled with something full and alive.

❧ Lucas' Defiance ❧

Lucas could feel the walls closing in. His father's conversations about leaving grew more frequent, and the weight of expectation hung heavy on his shoulders.

One afternoon, Lucas found himself in the garden, staring out across the expanse of green fields that stretched toward the horizon. Abeni was nearby, arranging flowers into a basket for Mrs. Sterling.

"Abeni," he called softly.

She turned, her eyes meeting his. There was something raw, something urgent in his gaze.

"I don't want to leave," he said, his voice trembling. "I don't want this to end."

Abeni stepped closer, clutching her basket to her chest. "Lucas, sometimes we cannot hold onto what is slipping away. We can only trust that God knows why."

He reached out, his hand gently brushing against hers. "But what if I don't want to trust? What if I want to fight?"

"Then fight," Abeni said softly. "But remember, love isn't always about holding on. Sometimes, it's about having the courage to let go."

❧ The Confrontation ❧

Mr. Sterling confronted Lucas in his study later that evening.

"You're spending too much time with that girl, Lucas. It's inappropriate, and it must stop."

Lucas stood tall, his voice steady. "Her name is Abeni, Father. And she's not just 'that girl.' She's... she's someone who's taught me more about life and faith than anything else here."

Mr. Sterling's expression softened briefly before hardening again. "This can't continue. We are leaving, Lucas. And you will not make this harder for your mother—or yourself."

Lucas turned away, his fists clenched at his sides.

Eleanor found Lucas in the family study, leaning over his sketchbook, charcoal smudges on his fingers. The evening light cast long shadows across the wooden floor.

"Lucas," she began softly, her voice carrying the weight of unspoken concern.

Lucas straightened but didn't meet her eyes. "Did you hear everything, Mother?"

Eleanor stepped forward, her heels silent on the carpet. "Enough to know that your heart is at war with itself."

Lucas exhaled sharply, closing the sketchbook. "He doesn't understand, Mother. He sees Nyathera as numbers on a ledger, but this place—it's alive. And Abeni... she's more than just a passing acquaintance."

Eleanor sat beside him, her eyes searching his face. "Your father... he fears losing you to a world he doesn't understand. But Lucas, love isn't always bound by what makes sense on paper."

Lucas looked at her, his voice breaking slightly. "And you? Do you understand?"

Eleanor smiled faintly, her fingers brushing his cheek. "I see you, Lucas. I see the light in your eyes when you speak of her, of this village. Follow that light, my son. Sometimes the most meaningful journeys begin with the courage to step away from expectations."

She stood, her silhouette framed by the evening glow. "But wherever you go, Lucas, let your heart remain true—to yourself, to Abeni, to the purpose God has written on your soul."

Lucas nodded, his throat tight. As Eleanor walked away, Lucas turned back to his sketchbook, his pencil trembling slightly in his hand.

The Unspoken Goodbye

Before dawn, Lucas stood by the garden gate one last time. The estate was still—no footsteps, no whispers, only the quiet breath of Nyathera wrapped in fog.

He held a small bundle of sketches—unfinished portraits of the village, the children at play, and one of Abeni, half-complete, the lines soft but sure.

He reached into his coat and pulled out a note. The parchment bore no declarations, just a simple sentence:

"In another life, I would have stayed. In this one, I must return before I can truly come home."

Lucas slipped it beneath a folded cloth on the worktable where Abeni often mentored village girls. She had once called the space "Threads of Hope"—not yet a building, but a dream stitched together with prayer and purpose.

He whispered to the space as if she could hear, *"One day, this will be more than a corner of your home. It will become what you've already named it."*

He turned toward the waiting carriage.

As the wheels creaked against the clay road, he looked back once—just once—toward the distant outline of the village. No one stirred. No one saw him go.

But somewhere in the stillness, a whisper seemed to carry through the morning breeze:

"Not all departures are loud. Some leave through silence, and still take your heart with them."

❧• Mama Tandiwe's Prayer •❧

The moment in the garden with Lucas felt like something sacred—fragile and full, as though the air itself had held its breath while their hearts spoke without saying too much. But even sacred moments end, and as the evening deepened, so did the weight in Abeni's chest.

That night, Abeni sat with Mama Tandiwe by the fire. The flames flickered, casting golden light across their faces and dancing shadows onto the clay walls of their small home. The pendant Lucas had placed around her neck rested quietly above her heart, its warmth still lingering. Abeni's hands lay in her lap, motionless, but her spirit felt restless—stirred by questions she couldn't yet name.

The sewing basket rested at Mama Tandiwe's feet, untouched. Instead, she stirred a pot of herbal tea with slow, thoughtful movements.

"Mama," Abeni said softly, her voice carrying the weight of questions too big for the silence, "why does love feel so heavy sometimes?"

Mama Tandiwe's eyes lifted toward her daughter, glinting with the quiet wisdom earned through years of both joy and sorrow. "Because real love carries the weight of truth, sacrifice, and hope, my child. But remember—love is never wasted, even if it doesn't end the way we imagine."

She reached out and took Abeni's hand. "God writes stories with threads we cannot always see. Trust Him, Abeni. Trust His plan."

Abeni lowered her gaze. Her fingers wrapped around the silver pendant at her neck, now warm from the nearness of her skin.

The fire crackled, and for a moment, neither of them spoke.

Then, with a soft hum, Mama Tandiwe began to sing—an old Shona hymn her husband used to hum while fixing fishing nets. It rose gently like incense, wrapping around the firelight:

"Mwari, ndibatei ruoko — mufambe neni, mumiyedzo yose..."
("Lord, hold my hand—walk with me through every trial...")

The melody was simple, familiar. Abeni joined in quietly, their voices braided in harmony, their song a bridge between generations.

When the last note faded into the silence, Mama Tandiwe closed her eyes and prayed aloud:

"Jehovah, we place this love in Your hands. Give Abeni the strength to carry what You've allowed, and the peace to surrender what she cannot hold. Guide her through the shadows, as You guided her father before her. May she walk in faith, not fear. Amen."

Abeni opened her eyes, blinking back tears.

"Love isn't always about holding on," Mama Tandiwe whispered again. "It's about having the courage to trust—even when the path ahead is clouded by storms."

The fire burned low, but the warmth between them remained—glowing, steady, and full of grace.

That night, under a sky strewn with stars, no goodbyes were spoken. No promises made. Just silence—thick, unspoken, and holy. By morning, Lucas was gone, and the village felt quieter than before, as if it too mourned what hadn't been said.

Mama Tandiwe's words echoed...

"Love isn't always about holding on—it's about having the
courage to trust, even when the path ahead
is clouded by storms."

CHAPTER SEVEN

HEALING AND HOPE

The sun had risen and set countless times since Lucas had left Nyathera, but Abeni could still feel the weight of his absence in the quiet moments—when the wind rustled the trees, or when the lantern light flickered in the stillness of night.

Life, however, did not stop. The village of Nyathera carried on with its timeless rhythm, and so did Abeni.

Threads of Purpose

The sewing corner in Abeni's small home had grown into something more—a place where other young women from the village would gather. They came with their own stories, their own pains, and their own hopes.

Though it was little more than a cleared space near the window, Abeni had begun to call it *"Threads of Hope."* The name came one quiet afternoon, when a young girl mending a torn dress asked if hope could be sewn into fabric. Abeni had smiled then and said, *"Everything we stitch carries something—why not hope too?"*

Under Mama Tandiwe's watchful eye, Abeni became a quiet mentor. She taught the girls not just how to stitch fabric, but how to stitch together the pieces of their lives.

One afternoon, as golden light poured through the small window, Abeni paused to watch the young women at work. Laughter rang out as one girl accidentally tangled her thread.

"Mama," Abeni said softly, "Sometimes I think the needle carries more than thread. It carries stories, hopes, and prayers."

Mama Tandiwe looked up from her stitching and smiled. "You're right, child. And every stitch you teach is a prayer answered for someone else."

Abeni's fingers tightened around the silver pendant Lucas had given her. It still hung around her neck, close to her heart.

∾• Letters Across the Sea •∾

Thousands of miles away, Lucas sat at his desk in a cramped apartment in Europe. The city was cold, gray, and impersonal—a sharp contrast to the warmth of Nyathera's golden sunsets and gentle breezes.

A stack of letters sat before him, many addressed to Abeni, yet never sent. His father had thrown himself into rebuilding their business, dragging Lucas into meetings, dinners, and responsibilities he had no passion for.

One evening, Lucas sat down with a blank sheet of paper and began to write:

"Dear Abeni,

Every day, I carry Nyathera with me—the scent of the flowers in the garden, the sound of your voice when you spoke my name, the strength in your eyes when you looked at me. Nothing here feels as real, as alive, as that place… as you.

I'm trying, Abeni. I'm trying to find a way back. Until then, know this: you are still the light that keeps me going.

Yours always,

Lucas"

He folded the letter carefully, but instead of sending it, he placed it in a drawer with the others.

∾• Village Rumors and Abeni's Faith •∾

Back in Nyathera, the whispers had not stopped. The village market, once a place of laughter and connection, felt different now.

"She still wears his pendant, you know," one woman muttered.

"As if he'll ever come back for her," another said with a dismissive shake of her head.

Abeni heard them, but she kept walking, her head held high. She had learned to silence the noise by focusing on the work of her hands and the whispers of her heart.

One evening, as the sky turned shades of amber and purple, Abeni sat by the riverbank where she often prayed.

"Lord," she whispered, her voice trembling, "if this love was only meant to be a season, let me carry it with grace. And if it is Your will... bring him back. But above all, let Your purpose be done."

A faint breeze stirred the water, carrying her prayer into the night.

☜· A Ray of Hope ·☞

Months later, a letter finally arrived for Abeni. It was handed to her by one of the village boys, the envelope slightly worn from travel.

Her hands shook as she opened it.

"Dear Abeni, I have found a way to return. It might not be soon, but it will happen. I am working hard to ensure that when I come back, I come back with purpose, with something to offer—not just to you, but to Nyathera. Please don't lose hope.

Yours always, Lucas"

Tears slipped down Abeni's cheeks as she pressed the letter to her chest. For the first time in months, she felt a fragile but undeniable hope stir within her.

☜· Mama Tandiwe's Blessing ·☞

That evening, Abeni shared the letter with Mama Tandiwe. The older woman read it carefully, her eyes soft with understanding.

"Abeni, child, love is a bridge built by faith. And sometimes, the hardest part is waiting for the other side to be finished."

Abeni nodded, her heart steady.

"Whatever happens, Mama, I trust God's plan."

"And that," Mama Tandiwe said softly, "is what makes you whole, my daughter. Your faith will carry you through every storm."

"Hope doesn't always come as a loud declaration—it often arrives quietly, folded into a letter, whispered in a prayer, or stitched into a simple piece of fabric."

CHAPTER EIGHT

THE RETURN

The sun hung low in the sky, casting golden rays across Nyathera. The village was alive with its usual sounds—children laughing, women bargaining at the market, and the distant hum of evening prayers. But today, there was something different in the air.

Abeni stood by the window, her sewing kit laid out before her, but her hands were still. A faint breeze stirred the curtains, carrying with it a familiar sound—the creak of carriage wheels on the clay road.

Her heart clenched, her breath hitching in her throat. She knew that sound.

ᴇ⌒• The Arrival •⌒ᴇ

The carriage came to a halt in the village square. Dust settled around it as the door swung open. For a moment, there was silence. And then Lucas stepped out.

His hair was slightly longer, his shoulders broader, and his eyes—oh, his eyes—carried the weight of journeys taken and promises kept.

The villagers had begun to gather at a distance, their whispers traveling like ripples on water.

"Is that the Sterling boy?"

"He's come back."

"What does he want now?"

But Lucas wasn't looking at them. His gaze swept across the crowd until it landed on Abeni, standing at the edge of the marketplace.

Abeni felt her feet move before her mind could catch up. The world blurred, and the only thing she could see was him.

When they stood face to face, words seemed insufficient. Lucas smiled softly, his voice a quiet tremor.

"I told you I'd come back."

Abeni nodded, tears brimming in her eyes. "And I kept believing you would."

∾• Conversations Rekindled •∾

Later, they sat under the familiar acacia tree—the same tree that had once witnessed quiet glances, awkward beginnings, and unspoken dreams.

Lucas reached into his satchel and pulled out a small bundle tied with a faded blue ribbon. The envelopes were worn, the edges yellowed with time, each one marked with her name in the unmistakable curve of his handwriting.

"I wrote you so many times, Abeni," he said, his voice low. "But I didn't always have the courage to send them. I kept writing... hoping."

Abeni stared at the bundle, her breath catching. She reached out slowly, her fingers trembling as they grazed the paper. The scent of aged parchment and distant memory clung to the pages.

With reverence, she held the letters close to her chest, as if cradling fragments of his heart.

"You came back, Lucas," she whispered. "That's what matters."

Lucas exhaled, his shoulders loosening as if shedding the years of absence.

"I'm not leaving again, Abeni. I've spoken to my parents. Things are different now. They've given me their blessing—though it wasn't easy. But I've also found my own path. I want to stay here... to help build something that lasts."

Abeni looked at him, her eyes glistening.

"And I will be here beside you, Lucas," she replied softly, the letters still pressed to her heart.

✎• A Village Divided •✎

Word of Lucas's return spread quickly through Nyathera. He walked beside Abeni through the village square the next morning, the sun casting soft shadows on the dusty paths. Some villagers greeted him with polite nods, others with narrowed eyes and cautious glances.

At the Threads of Hope display near the communal gathering space, a few children pointed in curiosity, while elders whispered behind shaded hands.

"Is that the Sterling boy?"

"Didn't he leave her without a word?"

"Why would he come back now?"

Later that week, Abeni and Lucas were seen together at the riverbank, laughing softly—an image that stirred both admiration and criticism. The village, long accustomed to silence and structure, now felt the ripple of something unexpected.

One afternoon, Abeni overheard two women near her workshop, their voices sharp and full of judgment.

"She's a fool to trust him again."

"Some people never learn."

Abeni's hands tightened around the fabric she was stitching. But before she could respond, Mama Tandiwe appeared beside her, her voice steady and strong.

"Child, love is often misunderstood by those who've never dared to risk it. Hold your head high and let your actions speak louder than their words."

Abeni nodded, her heart steadying under her mother's wisdom.

✎• Lucas' Reflection •✎

Though the old Sterling homestead had remained locked and silent since their departure, Lucas had chosen simpler lodgings—a modest clay-walled hut at the edge of the village, not far from the riverbank. It had once belonged to the village's late potter, and with the elder's council's blessing, he had restored it with his own hands.

Most mornings, he could be found helping rebuild community benches, sketching designs for the school's broken shutters, or sitting with children beneath the shade of the baobab tree, teaching them how to draw with charcoal. He moved through Nyathera quietly—less as the foreign heir, and more as a man seeking to earn his place with humility.

As twilight deepened over Nyathera, Lucas stood on the veranda of Abeni's sewing workshop. The soft glow of lantern light spilled onto the clay ground, and somewhere nearby, children's laughter carried on the breeze. Yet Lucas' thoughts were elsewhere—back in the study of his family's home, on the day he decided to return.

It had been a gray afternoon, rain tapping softly against the windowpane. Mr. Sterling sat behind his grand mahogany desk, papers scattered before him. Lucas stood across from him, his hands clenched into fists at his sides.

"Are you certain about this, Lucas?" Mr. Sterling's voice was steady, but his eyes carried a weight Lucas had not often seen—a father's quiet fear of letting go.

"Yes, Father," Lucas said, his voice resolute. "Nyathera isn't just a chapter in my story—it's home. And Abeni... she's my heart."

Mr. Sterling leaned back in his chair, his brow furrowed in thought. "You're choosing a difficult path, son. Love across divides—of culture, expectation, and history—it's not an easy road to walk."

Lucas' jaw tightened, but he held his father's gaze. "I'd rather walk a difficult road with her than an easy one without her."

There was a long silence before Mr. Sterling sighed deeply, rubbing his temples. When he finally spoke, his voice was softer.

"Then make sure you honor that, Lucas. Don't let your intentions falter. Love is not just a feeling—it's a choice you make every day. And it's a promise you must keep, no matter the storms that come."

Lucas swallowed the knot in his throat. "I will, Father."

For a brief moment, something unspoken passed between them—an understanding, fragile but sincere.

The memory faded as Lucas returned to the present moment, the scent of earth and lantern smoke grounding him in Nyathera. He exhaled slowly, his resolve solidifying.

"I chose this path," he thought. *"And I'll walk it with honor."*

∾• A Promise Rekindled •∾

One evening, under the same stars that had once witnessed their goodbyes, Lucas and Abeni stood side by side.

Lucas reached for Abeni's hand, his voice trembling with emotion.

"I came back not just because I love you, Abeni, but because I believe in what we can build together. Will you let me walk this road with you, hand in hand, for however long God allows us?"

Abeni's eyes shimmered with tears, but her smile was radiant.

"Yes, Lucas. With all my heart, yes."

The wind whispered through the trees, and the silver pendant around Abeni's neck caught the moonlight—a symbol of love that had endured the test of time and distance.

"Sometimes, love doesn't return with grand fanfare—it arrives quietly, humbly, and with a heart ready to rebuild what was once broken."

CHAPTER Nine

BUILDING TOGETHER

The sun dipped low over Nyathera as the rhythmic sound of hammers striking wood and the joyful chatter of busy hands filled the air. The once-empty plot beside Mama Tandiwe's home was slowly being transformed into something more than a structure—it was becoming a sanctuary of dreams. They called it *House of Threads*, a name whispered into being by the women whose stitches had mended more than fabric.

Lucas stood beside Abeni, their hands dusted with sawdust and their faces streaked with the glow of hard work. Though he now stayed in the old potter's hut just beyond the stream, he spent most of his waking hours here, helping bring Abeni's vision to life.

They had gathered a community—village men lifting beams onto their shoulders, women dyeing cloth and stitching vibrant banners, and children running with paintbrushes dipped in brilliant hues, turning the clay walls into stories.

"It's coming together," Abeni said softly, her voice carrying a note of wonder.

Lucas nodded, wiping sweat from his brow. "It is. And it's because of you, Abeni. Your vision, your faith—it's contagious."

Abeni smiled, though her eyes drifted toward the path leading back to the market. "But not everyone believes in this, Lucas. Not everyone believes in… us."

Lucas exhaled, his hand finding hers. "Then let's show them, Abeni. Let's show them what love and purpose can build."

∽• A Rift in the Village •∽

Despite the progress, the village was not entirely united in its support. Elder Jabari had offered his blessing, but the whispers lingered—clinging to fence posts, drifting between market stalls, and curling into corners of doubt.

One afternoon, as Abeni guided a group of young women beneath a canvas tent, teaching them new embroidery techniques, two older women approached the edge of the gathering.

"You think this will last, Abeni?" one of them said, arms crossed. "You think this... partnership with him will hold?"

Abeni paused, her hands stilling on the fabric she was stitching. She looked up, calm and unflinching.

"It's not just a partnership," she said. "It's a vision—a purpose planted by God. And we're working, day by day, to honor that."

The women exchanged glances but said nothing more, walking away with their baskets tucked close to their chests.

From across the clearing, Mama Tandiwe stood watching, her eyes filled with quiet pride. The threads that held her daughter's courage together were not easily snapped.

∽• Lucas' Letter from Home •∽

That evening, just after the last nail had been hammered into place for the day, Lucas sat by the riverbank—the same one where he had once watched the sunset as a stranger to Nyathera, now flowing beside him like an old companion. In his hands, he held a letter, its edges worn and creased by many rereads.

Abeni joined him, her skirt brushing softly against the tall reeds. She sat beside him without a word, her presence folding gently into the quiet.

"Is it from your parents?" she asked, sensing the way his thumb lingered on the parchment.

Lucas nodded. "From my mother. She writes more often now. My father remains… guarded. But he no longer asks her to stop."

He hesitated for a moment, then unfolded the letter and read aloud, his voice low and steady:

Lucas, my son,

I see glimpses of who you are becoming in every word you write to me. Your letters carry something deeper than defiance—they carry purpose. I still struggle to understand your choice, but I can no longer deny the conviction in your voice. Your father may not say it, but he sees it too. We both do.

Keep building, Lucas. Build something we will one day be proud to see with our own eyes.

Lucas lowered the page, his gaze tracing the surface of the river. "She's beginning to understand," he whispered.

Abeni reached over and placed her hand gently on his shoulder. "Sometimes love begins with understanding, Lucas. And sometimes… it ends with it."

He nodded, the tension in his jaw softening. "I didn't want to stay in the Sterling homestead," he said after a pause. "It felt too grand… too far removed from the life we're trying to build."

"So you chose the old potter's hut," Abeni said quietly.

Lucas smiled faintly. "It was abandoned, but with a bit of cleaning, it became enough. It reminds me that I'm not here to be served—I'm here to serve."

He paused, then added, "I used some of my own savings from university work—editing academic papers, translating documents. It's not much, but enough for now. And once the workshop opens fully, I want to create a space where others can learn a skill, earn a living. It has to be more than just about us."

Abeni's eyes shimmered as the last light of the sun kissed the horizon. "Then you're already richer than most."

The river rustled beside them, carrying away the silence and replacing it with a quiet sense of belonging. The weight of legacy and love, purpose and uncertainty, sat between them—but so did hope.

An Unexpected Incident

Just as the final beams were being secured and walls took on their shape, the village's heartbeat quickened with anticipation—but so did its risks.

One late afternoon, as the golden sun cast long shadows across the building site, a loud crash split the air. A wooden beam had slipped from a scaffold, landing dangerously close to where a group of young boys had been passing buckets of water.

Lucas was the first to react, rushing forward, his voice firm but composed. "Is everyone alright?"

The youngest boy, shaken but unharmed, clung to an older sibling. Murmurs rose around them like smoke.

The boy's father pushed through the crowd, eyes blazing. "We can't risk our children here, Lucas! This project—it's not worth their safety!"

Lucas raised both hands, steady and calm. "I understand your concern. And I agree—nothing is worth risking their lives. We will review everything—every structure, every process. I promise."

Just then, Abeni arrived, breathless, a shadow of fear crossing her otherwise steady gaze. She knelt to check the boys, her hands gentle, mother-like.

"This place is meant to be," she said, standing slowly. "But only if we build it together—with care, with wisdom, with love."

The father hesitated. The crowd was silent, watching him, waiting.

Finally, he exhaled, his jaw loosening. "We'll try again. But only if you keep that promise."

Lucas nodded. "We will. Starting tomorrow morning, we double-check every beam and every rope. No shortcuts."

As the crowd began to disperse, Abeni turned to Lucas, her voice hushed. "That was too close."

Lucas wrapped an arm around her shoulders, pulling her close. "We'll do better, Abeni. We're still learning… but we won't give up. Not now."

Above them, the evening wind whispered through the trees as if affirming their vow—fragile yet unbroken.

☙• A Quiet Reckoning •❧

That night, the village exhaled slowly, returning to stillness after the day's commotion. The hum of insects rose again, weaving with the distant bark of a dog and the rustle of wind in the trees.

Abeni sat quietly on the small bench outside her mother's home, her back resting against the mud-plastered wall. The flickering light of the nearby fire pit danced across her features, which were taut with lingering tension. Her hands lay in her lap, unmoving—save for the thumb that nervously traced the edge of her silver pendant.

She replayed the moment the beam fell—the startled cry, the rush of feet, the accusing glances. The closeness of disaster still trembled in her chest.

From a distance, she could hear Lucas's voice mingling with the elders as he reviewed the safety measures once more. He was thorough, determined—but even his diligence couldn't fully quiet the questions in her heart.

"We're building more than walls," she whispered to the night sky, the words catching in her throat like a prayer.

Moments later, she rose, pushing open the wooden door to find Mama Tandiwe waiting—her needle poised mid-stitch, as if she already knew her daughter would need more than words.

Mama Tandiwe's Wisdom

Inside, the familiar scent of herbs and woodsmoke greeted Abeni like a warm embrace. Mama Tandiwe glanced up as her daughter entered, then quietly set her sewing aside.

Without a word, Abeni sank down beside her, resting her head gently against her mother's shoulder—seeking refuge, and perhaps, reassurance.

"Mama," she said at last, her voice barely above a whisper, "what if this all falls apart? What if the doubts, the whispers, the mistakes—what if they're right?"

Mama Tandiwe took Abeni's hands into her own weathered palms, her touch firm yet tender. The fire crackled softly, casting dancing shadows on the walls as if echoing the truths about to be spoken.

"Child," she began gently, "every great thing that was ever built started with doubt. Every story of faith began with fear. But what separates those who stop from those who see it through... is courage."

Abeni nodded slowly, her eyes glassy, but no longer heavy with despair.

"And remember, Abeni," Mama Tandiwe said, pressing their joined hands to her chest, "God does not give us visions He does not intend to fulfill. Walk by faith, my child, and let Him do the rest."

Views of the World and Legacies

Far away from the lantern-lit evenings of Nyathera, in the heart of the city, James Sterling stood by the tall window of his study. The glow of the setting sun bathed the room in amber, but his gaze was fixed beyond the horizon—beyond what he could control.

On the edge of his polished mahogany desk lay a neat pile of letters—each one penned in his son's handwriting. Letters filled with details of village life, of bricks being laid and cloth being stitched, of challenges faced and quiet joys discovered.

James picked one up, his fingers brushing the worn edges. He had read each line more times than he cared to admit.

"He should be here," he murmured, almost to himself. "At my side. Learning how to carry this legacy forward."

But even as the words left his mouth, something inside him faltered. Lucas had always been different—drawn not to power, but to people. Where James saw transactions, Lucas saw transformation.

His thoughts drifted to the old conversation they once had: *"You have a romantic view of the world, son. Business isn't about sentimentality."*

Yet now, standing in the quiet ache of a father's reflection, James wasn't so sure.

"Perhaps," he whispered, "I've spent too long trying to shape him in my image, when he was always meant to build his own."

A gentle knock interrupted his thoughts. The door opened, and Eleanor entered, her presence soft, grounding.

"You're thinking about him again," she said, stepping beside him.

James didn't turn to face her. "He's chosen a path I never envisioned for him. I just hope it doesn't... break him."

Eleanor placed a steady hand on his arm. "Or perhaps, James... he's choosing the very path that will make him whole."

A long silence followed, filled only by the ticking of the old wall clock. Then, without speaking, James rested his hand over hers—a fragile sign that her words had landed.

Outside, the sky shifted from gold to indigo, as if heaven itself were painting a canvas of grace, change, and the quiet beauty of letting go. Weaving a tapestry of grace and acceptance.

CHAPTER Ten

When Rain Falls

The skies over Nyathera darkened with the promise of rain. The air was thick with anticipation, as if the heavens themselves were holding their breath. In the distance, thunder rolled softly—a low hum that stirred both awe and unease.

Abeni stood beneath the baobab tree, her eyes lifted toward the gathering clouds. The scent of wet earth rose around her, mingling with the memories of all they had built, all they had dared to believe.

The workshop was nearly complete. The banners had been hung. Shelves were stacked with vibrant fabrics, and laughter had begun to echo again through the village pathways. Yet a tension lingered—unspoken, unnamed, but present.

Lucas arrived at her side, rain-speckled and breathless, having just come from a visit with Elder Jabari.

"He wants to bless the centre," Lucas said, wiping his forehead with the sleeve of his tunic. "He said he's watched us build—not just the walls, but trust."

Abeni smiled faintly, though her fingers twisted nervously at the hem of her wrap. "And yet some still wait for it to crumble."

Lucas reached for her hand. "Then let it rain, Abeni. Let the heavens test what we've planted. We'll see what takes root."

A few drops began to fall—gentle at first, then steadier, until the sky wept freely. Villagers ran for shelter, but Abeni and Lucas remained, drenched, their faces lifted to the storm.

They didn't run. They didn't hide.

They stood.

Together.

Because sometimes the rain didn't mean destruction.

Sometimes, the rain meant blessing.

Sometimes, it meant cleansing.

Sometimes, it simply meant… growth.

Later that evening, after the rain had stopped, villagers trickled out of their homes—some to check on the structure, others simply to see what remained. To their quiet surprise, the *Threads of Hope* workshop stood firm, the painted signs unblurred, the fabric banners drying gently in the wind.

Mama Tandiwe stepped quietly into the middle of the courtyard, her shawl wrapped loosely around her shoulders. She gazed upward at the clearing sky and spoke with calm authority:

"What God ordains, no storm can erase."

Her words floated through the air like incense, carried by the breeze—and heard.

The next morning, as mist lingered low over the hills, small offerings began to appear outside the workshop. A basket of sweet potatoes. A hand-carved stool. Fresh flowers. Pieces of fabric from families who had once stood at a distance.

They said nothing.

But they left something.

And in Nyathera, that meant everything.

CHAPTER Eleven

A Shared Future

The sky above Nyathera was painted in soft hues of lavender and gold as the sun dipped low on the horizon. The village square was alive with quiet anticipation, the air filled with the scent of fresh flowers and spices. Colorful banners fluttered in the gentle breeze, and lanterns hung like stars from tree branches, casting a warm glow over the Threads of Hope workshop.

It was a day the village would remember—a day of celebration, gratitude, and renewal.

❧ The Inauguration Ceremony ☙

Elder Jabari stood at the front of the courtyard, his staff firmly planted in the ground beside him. The crowd gathered around him—mothers holding infants, children peeking curiously from behind their elders, young women wearing dresses they had sewn with their own hands.

Lucas and Abeni stood together near the entrance of the workshop. Lucas was dressed in a crisp white shirt and light brown trousers, his hair tousled slightly by the wind. Abeni wore a soft yellow dress she had stitched herself, delicate vines embroidered along the sleeves and hem. Her pendant rested above her heart, catching the sunlight with each breath.

Elder Jabari raised his hands, his deep voice carrying over the crowd.

"Today, we gather not just to celebrate the opening of a building, but to honor the spirit with which it was built. This place, Threads of Hope, is more than wood and nails—it is a promise. A promise that no one is forgotten, no story is insignificant, and no future is beyond redemption."

The crowd murmured in agreement, some wiping away tears, others clutching the hands of their loved ones.

He turned towards Abeni and Lucas.

"You have both given us more than a workshop—you've given us a vision. A vision of what happens when love, faith, and purpose come together. May this place stand not only as a shelter but as a bridge—a bridge between hearts, between dreams, and between what is and what can be."

The crowd erupted in applause, cheers ringing through the air. Lucas and Abeni exchanged a glance, their hands clasped tightly together.

"Sometimes, the greatest structures are not built with bricks and mortar, but with love, faith, and hands willing to keep building even when the world says stop."

A Shared Reflection

As the ceremony transitioned into a vibrant celebration, villagers shared food, laughter, and music. Children chased one another through the courtyard, their joy infectious.

Lucas and Abeni stepped away from the crowd, finding a quiet corner under the acacia tree. The warm golden light of the setting sun painted their faces.

"This feels like a dream," Abeni whispered, her eyes scanning the bustling scene before them.

Lucas smiled, his gaze fixed on her. "It's not a dream, Abeni. It's a promise kept. And it's only the beginning."

Abeni turned to him, her eyes glistening with unshed tears. "Do you ever wonder, Lucas... if we had taken different paths, if we had let fear hold us back, would we still have found our way here?"

Lucas shook his head gently. "No. Every moment, every choice, every prayer—it led us here. And I wouldn't trade this for anything."

Their hands remained intertwined, a silent vow passing between them.

In the distance, Mama Tandiwe watched them from her seat beside the workshop door, her heart full and her spirit at peace.

❧ Seeds of Tomorrow ❧

Later that evening, as the celebration wound down and lanterns cast soft pools of light across the courtyard, Lucas found himself walking through the workshop, running his fingers lightly over bolts of fabric and carefully arranged spools of thread.

Abeni joined him, her bare feet making no sound on the polished floor.

"You look deep in thought," she said softly.

Lucas turned, his expression both serious and tender. "This place, Abeni... it's a living prayer. Every stitch, every seam—it tells a story. But it's only just beginning."

Abeni stepped closer, her voice steady. "We'll build it, Lucas. Together."

Lucas reached into his pocket and pulled out a folded piece of parchment. "There's something I wanted to show you."

He handed her the paper. It was a sketch—a drawing of an expanded Threads of Hope workshop, with additional rooms for training, a library, and a space for children to play and learn.

Abeni's breath caught as she traced the lines with her fingertips. "Lucas... this is beautiful."

"It's our next step," he said quietly. "If you'll build it with me."

Abeni looked up, her smile radiant. "Always."

❧ Under the Starlit Sky ❧

The night had fully fallen over Nyathera by the time Lucas and Abeni stepped outside. The sky was a blanket of stars, stretching endlessly above them.

"You know," Lucas began, his voice low, "I used to think legacy was about wealth, power, and numbers in a ledger. But it's not, is it?"

Abeni shook her head softly. "No, Lucas. Legacy is about love. It's about what we build with our hands and leave behind in the hearts of others."

Lucas turned to face her fully, his blue-gray eyes reflecting the starlight. "Then let's make sure this legacy lasts, Abeni. For them, for us, for the generations that will come after."

They stood together in silence for a moment, listening to the sounds of the village settling into the quiet of the night.

Above them, the stars shimmered—a silent witness to promises made, love shared, and a future unfolding with every heartbeat.

"Sometimes, the most profound beginnings are not marked by grand gestures, but by quiet promises made under starlit skies, with hands intertwined and hearts aligned in purpose."

CHAPTER *Twelve*

THE

PROPOSAL

The days after the Threads of Hope inauguration were filled with a quiet sense of fulfillment. The workshop buzzed with life and purpose as women stitched patterns into vibrant fabrics, children played in the courtyard, and the hum of sewing machines created a soft rhythm that echoed hope.

But amidst the beauty of it all, Lucas carried something in his pocket—a small velvet box, its weight both comforting and daunting. The time had come to take the next step.

A Quiet Plan

Lucas paced near the acacia tree, the very spot where so many meaningful conversations with Abeni had unfolded. He rolled the velvet box between his fingers, his chest rising and falling with steady breaths.

Mama Tandiwe approached quietly, her shawl draped over her shoulders. "Lucas," she said gently, her voice carrying its usual warmth, "you've been wearing out the grass under this tree all morning."

Lucas chuckled nervously, rubbing the back of his neck. "Mama Tandiwe, I—I'm not sure if I'll find the right words."

Mama Tandiwe smiled, her eyes twinkling. "When love speaks, Lucas, the right words find you. Trust your heart."

She gave his arm a reassuring squeeze before walking back towards the workshop, leaving Lucas alone under the ancient branches.

⁓· The Riverbank – A Moment Stitched in Eternity ·⁓

The sky above Nyathera was painted in hues of twilight—deep purples and soft golds blending like watercolors on an endless canvas. The river flowed steadily, its surface shimmering under the tender glow of the fading sun. Abeni stood at the edge of the riverbank, her shawl wrapped tightly around her shoulders as the evening breeze whispered secrets through the trees.

She had come here to think, to pray, to breathe. The river had always been her sanctuary, a place where her thoughts could run free like the water before her. But tonight, something felt different—almost expectant, as if the air itself was holding its breath.

The sound of approaching footsteps made her turn slowly. There, emerging from the shadows of the acacia trees, was Lucas. His figure was illuminated softly by the remaining light of the sunset, and his eyes—those blue-gray eyes that had seen her soul—held a mixture of vulnerability and quiet determination.

"Lucas," Abeni said softly, her voice carrying over the gentle murmur of the river.

He stepped closer, his hands tucked into his coat pockets as if holding something fragile. "I hoped I'd find you here," he said, his voice low but steady.

Abeni offered a faint smile. "You always seem to know where to find me."

For a moment, they stood in silence, the weight of unspoken words suspended between them. Lucas took a deep breath, his gaze fixed on her as if he was memorizing every detail of her face—the curve of her smile, the way her hair caught the faint light, the quiet strength in her eyes.

"I remember the first time I saw you," he began, his voice soft but firm. "You were standing outside the marketplace, holding a basket filled with fabric. There was a kindness in your eyes, Abeni—something I couldn't look away from. And then... there were the little moments. The way you spoke about your dreams, the way you stitched hope into every garment, the way you carried faith in your heart even when everything felt uncertain."

Abeni's eyes shimmered with tears as he spoke.

"Do you know how many times I've imagined this moment?" Lucas continued, his voice catching slightly. "When we were apart—when the world felt impossibly vast between us—I would close my eyes and picture you here, standing by this river, with the light catching in your eyes. And every time, Abeni, every single time, I would promise myself that if I ever got the chance... if I ever got to stand here with you again... I wouldn't let the moment slip away."

He took a step closer, the distance between them now almost nonexistent. Slowly, he reached into his pocket and pulled out a small velvet box. His hands trembled slightly as he opened it, revealing a delicate ring that glinted softly in the twilight.

"This ring isn't just a piece of jewelry," Lucas said, his voice barely above a whisper, yet every word carried weight. "It's a promise. A promise to stand beside you, to honor you, and to build a life with you—not just in the good days, but in every storm and every sunrise. It's a symbol of every prayer I've whispered, every dream I've dared to believe, and every moment I've longed for this day."

Abeni's breath hitched, her tears spilling freely now as her hand flew to her mouth.

Lucas knelt down, one knee pressing into the soft earth, and looked up at her with eyes filled with love and vulnerability.

"Abeni," he said, his voice steady despite the emotion trembling beneath it. "Will you walk with me—not just here, not just tonight—but through every valley, every storm, and every joy? Will you let me love you, honor you, and cherish you for all the days we are given?"

Abeni's shoulders shook with quiet sobs as she lowered herself to her knees, their faces now level, their tears mingling in the glow of the fading light.

"Yes," she whispered, her voice trembling yet clear. "Yes, Lucas. A thousand times yes."

A tear slipped down Lucas' cheek as he carefully slipped the ring onto her finger. His hands lingered there, holding hers as if anchoring them both to this sacred moment.

For a heartbeat—or perhaps an eternity—they stayed that way. The river murmured softly, the stars began to blink awake in the sky, and the breeze carried the scent of wildflowers through the air.

Lucas pulled Abeni into his arms, holding her as though the world itself was stitched together by their embrace. And in that quiet, holy moment under the watchful sky and the flowing river, love became not just a feeling, but a sacred covenant.

Above them, the first stars of the evening flickered to life, and somewhere in the stillness, a whisper seemed to linger on the wind:

"Love is the thread that binds us, and in this moment, eternity is stitched into every heartbeat."

Reflections Under Moonlight

The walk home felt both endless and fleeting. The silver ring on Abeni's finger seemed to carry the weight of every whispered prayer she had ever uttered. As the lanterns of their home came into view, she paused for a moment under the star-strewn sky, clutching the pendant Lucas had given her.

Her heart felt full—overflowing, even—but there was an ache there too, an ache born from the gravity of the moment. *What does it mean to love someone this deeply? To promise forever in a world so fragile?*

Inside, Mama Tandiwe was seated near the flickering oil lamp, her sewing needle paused mid-air as she looked up at her daughter. Abeni's smile was soft, secretive—a light barely contained.

"Mama, I… I'll tell you everything in the morning," Abeni said gently, her voice trembling with emotions she wasn't yet ready to unpack aloud.

Mama Tandiwe studied her daughter's face and saw the quiet glow in her eyes, the way her shoulders were no longer weighed down by uncertainty. She nodded and rose from her chair.

"Alright, my child. Rest now."

But Abeni hardly slept. She lay awake, her fingers brushing the silver ring as the night air carried the faint hum of crickets into her room. She whispered silent prayers, gratitude pouring from her heart like an overflowing cup.

Across the village, Lucas too found himself staring at the moonlit sky. He leaned against the balcony railing of the Sterling estate, the distant outline of the Threads of Hope workshop barely visible in the darkness.

This is what I've waited for. This moment, this promise.

But with joy came an unspoken weight—a responsibility. *Can I truly be the man she deserves? Can I protect this love, nurture it, and build something lasting?*

Sleep came to neither of them easily that night, but as dawn painted the sky in soft hues of gold and lavender, both Abeni and Lucas felt a quiet peace settle in their hearts.

❧ Sharing the News ☙

The morning sun filtered through the leaves of the acacia tree, casting golden patterns on the courtyard where Abeni stood quietly, her fingers brushing the smooth silver of the ring. She had waited for the right moment—one sacred enough to carry the weight of the promise now encircling her finger.

Mama Tandiwe sat near the clay hearth, sorting herbs into woven baskets. Her presence, grounded and serene, felt like the earth itself—steady, seasoned, and full of secrets.

Abeni walked slowly toward her mother, her heart pounding with joy and reverence. She knelt beside her, holding out her hand so the light caught the gentle glint of the ring.

"Mama," she said softly, barely above a whisper, "Lucas asked me to marry him."

The herbs slipped through Mama Tandiwe's fingers as her eyes filled with tears. She looked at the ring, then at Abeni's face—bright with love, yet softened by awe.

She reached out, her calloused hands cupping Abeni's cheeks, and drew her daughter into an embrace that felt like home.

"My child," she murmured, her voice trembling, "my precious Abeni. You are becoming a wife."

They held each other, tears flowing freely—tears of memory, of hope, and of silent prayers answered in time.

After a long pause, Mama Tandiwe pulled back, her gaze now distant, resting somewhere in memory.

"Your father proposed to me beneath the old baobab," she said, her voice a melody of nostalgia. "He had no ring, just a promise and eyes that carried dreams too big for his pockets. I said yes, not to a future I could see, but to a man who made me feel seen. And now here you are, loved in a way that honors your worth."

Abeni's eyes brimmed again. "I wanted to tell you first, Mama. Before we tell anyone else. Because your blessing means the world to me."

Mama Tandiwe smiled, her eyes crinkling at the corners. "Then you have it, my daughter. And may this love be as enduring as the river's song— sometimes quiet, sometimes fierce, but always flowing."

They sat for a while in the stillness, the morning breeze rustling the trees above them. Abeni leaned her head against her mother's shoulder, the rhythm of their heartbeats echoing the generations of women before them.

And though Lucas waited nearby, he would hear of the blessing soon enough. For now, it was a moment reserved for mother and daughter—a sacred space where love, memory, and legacy met.

ᐤᖷᐧ *A Mother's Blessing* ·ᐤᖷ

Later that afternoon, as the sun stretched golden across the courtyard and the scent of simmering herbs danced in the air, Lucas made his way toward the homestead. His steps were steady but reverent, each one echoing the weight of the commitment he had made.

He paused at the threshold of Mama Tandiwe's home, brushing the dust from his boots and smoothing the creases in his shirt. In his hands, he carried a small bundle—a woven cloth wrapped around two carved wooden figurines and a pouch of fragrant incense, symbols of goodwill and respect from his homeland.

Mama Tandiwe met him at the doorway, her eyes warm and welcoming.

"Lucas," she greeted with a small smile, stepping aside. "It's good to see you. Come in, come in."

He entered slowly, offering a slight bow of respect before taking a seat where she gestured.

"I trust the walk over wasn't too long," she added as she poured him a cup of honeyed tea.

Lucas accepted it with both hands, grateful. "Thank you, Mama Tandiwe. The air was fresh—it gave me time to reflect."

They sat for a moment in a comfortable stillness, the distant sound of birdsong filling the space between them.

Then, Lucas glanced up. "Has Abeni spoken to you yet?"

"She has," Mama Tandiwe said softly, her eyes gleaming. "I saw the light in her eyes before she even said a word."

Lucas let out a breath he hadn't realized he was holding.

"I wanted to come today to seek your counsel," he said earnestly. "I want to do this the right way... the respectful way. What are the customary steps I need to follow to honour you, the family, and the traditions that shaped Abeni?"

She studied him for a moment, her eyes searching not for words but for the sincerity behind them.

"You've done well to ask, son," she said, pouring him a cup of honeyed tea. "Love may begin in the heart, but marriage lives in the soil of family and tradition. There are elders to consult, customs to observe, prayers to be said. This is not just about you and Abeni—it is about the weaving together of two lineages."

Lucas leaned in, absorbing every word.

"I will guide you," Mama Tandiwe continued. "There is no shame in learning the ways of a people if your heart is willing. And from what I've seen, yours is."

She then rose, placed her hands gently on his shoulders, and spoke a quiet blessing in her native tongue—words of protection, honor, and wisdom.

A soft rustle behind them drew Mama Tandiwe's attention toward the doorway. Abeni stood quietly, her silhouette framed by the warm afternoon light, her hands gently clasped at her waist.

She stepped forward slowly, her voice tender and filled with emotion.

"I didn't mean to interrupt. I just wanted to… be here."

Mama Tandiwe smiled and reached out her hand, beckoning her daughter.

"Come, my child. This moment is yours, too."

Together, the three moved to the old acacia tree—a place that had witnessed many seasons of their lives. Its branches arched overhead like an embrace, casting a sacred hush over the gathering.

Mama Tandiwe took a deep breath, then turned to a small wooden box she had carried with her. From it, she withdrew a delicate beaded bracelet, its colours faded but its thread still strong.

"This was given to me by your father on the day he came to seek my hand," she said, her eyes misty with memory. "It has held the prayers of our beginnings… and now, I pass it to you, Abeni, as a symbol of blessing and continuity."

She fastened the bracelet around her daughter's wrist, then placed a hand on each of their shoulders.

"This union," she said softly, "has heaven's fingerprint on it. I bless you both—not only for who you are, but for what you will become together."

As they stood in quiet reverence beneath the old tree, the breeze stirred its branches gently, scattering a few golden leaves to the ground—nature's silent benediction upon love's sacred covenant.

୧୬• Village Whispers •୨୧

Word of the engagement spread quickly through Nyathera. Some villagers rejoiced, their smiles bright and their congratulations heartfelt. But others whispered behind cupped hands and cast sideways glances, like shadows unwilling to fade in the light.

"Do you think it will last?"

"A union like this... it's not natural."

"They're from two different worlds."

Abeni heard the murmurs as she walked through the marketplace, her engagement ring catching the sunlight like a quiet defiance. She kept her head high, but the weight of their words gathered like dust on her spirit—soft, persistent, and suffocating.

One afternoon, as she and Lucas walked near the Threads of Hope workshop, her silence said more than words.

"They're talking, aren't they?" Lucas asked softly.

Abeni paused, then nodded. "Yes. But Lucas... their words don't change my heart. God brought us here, to this moment. And I will trust Him with the rest."

Lucas reached for her hand, his voice calm and steady. "And we'll face it together, Abeni. Every whisper, every doubt—we'll walk through it, side by side."

As they continued walking, the wind rustled through the jacaranda trees, scattering purple petals along their path. And though the voices around them grew louder, Abeni and Lucas held fast to a truth that was louder still—love, anchored in purpose, would outlast every storm.

"Let them whisper—for love that is rooted in grace does not tremble in the wind, but grows deeper with every storm it survives."

CHAPTER Thirteen

A Family's Shadow

⊷· A Troubled Past Unveiled ·⊷

The night was heavy with silence, broken only by the faint creak of the wooden floorboards as Abeni walked into the main room of their small home. Mama Tandiwe sat by the flickering light of the oil lamp, her sewing resting idly in her lap.

"Mama," Abeni said softly, hesitating near the doorway. "Can we talk?"

Mama Tandiwe looked up, her face etched with lines carved by time and unspoken sorrows. She gestured for Abeni to sit beside her.

"There's something I should have told you long ago, Abeni," Mama Tandiwe began, her voice trembling slightly. "The night your father disappeared... I remember it as if it were yesterday. He had gone out on his boat—he was always so confident on the water. But that night, the winds were fierce, and the river's current was angry."

Abeni listened intently, her hands folded tightly in her lap.

"For days, we searched," Mama Tandiwe continued. "When his boat was found downstream, empty and splintered, the whispers began. They said... they said I had something to do with it. That I had bewitched him, that I had driven him into the storm."

Tears glistened in Mama Tandiwe's eyes as her voice faltered. "Some of the elders refused to listen when I pleaded my innocence. They turned their backs on me, on us. For years, I carried the weight of their accusations, the shame they placed on our family."

Abeni's throat tightened, her voice a faint whisper. "Why didn't you ever tell me this, Mama?"

"Because I didn't want you to carry this burden," Mama Tandiwe said firmly. "But now, as you prepare to step into a new life with Lucas, you need to understand... love does not silence whispers, but it does give us the strength to rise above them."

❧ Threads of Judgment ·❧

The following morning, Abeni wandered through the Threads of Hope workshop, her thoughts heavy with the revelations of the previous night. Each stitch she made felt like a fragile prayer, each pull of the needle a whispered hope.

Lucas found her there, seated by a window, sunlight casting soft patterns across her face.

"Abeni?" he said gently, kneeling beside her. "Your eyes... they carry a weight I haven't seen before."

Abeni hesitated, her hands clutching a spool of thread. "Lucas, my family... we've carried shadows. The whispers of the village—they're not just about us. They're about my father, about my mother. About me."

Lucas reached for her hand, his voice steady and sure. "Abeni, your past doesn't define your worth. And neither do their whispers. What matters is what we choose to build together."

Tears welled in Abeni's eyes, but she nodded, finding strength in his unwavering gaze.

"Whatever shadows exist," Lucas continued, his thumb brushing over her knuckles, "we'll face them together. No whisper, no shadow, no past will take away what we have."

❧ A Moment of Comfort ·❧

That evening, as the village settled into quiet, Lucas sat with Mama Tandiwe outside their home, the sky painted in dusky hues.

"Mama Tandiwe," Lucas began hesitantly, "I wanted to ask... is there anything I should know before we take this step? Anything about the past that could cast doubt on our future?"

Mama Tandiwe sighed deeply, her eyes reflecting the glow of the lantern beside them.

"Lucas, love is not just about facing the future—it's also about making peace with the past. Yes, there have been shadows, accusations, and pain. But Abeni... she carries light in her spirit, light that no shadow can extinguish."

She paused, then added thoughtfully, "You asked me once about our customs—the ways of honouring family, community, and legacy. In our tradition, marriage is not only a joining of hearts, but of histories. It is not enough to carry love; you must also carry understanding."

Lucas nodded slowly, his jaw set with quiet determination. "I promise you, Mama Tandiwe, I will honor her light. I will cherish it, protect it, and let it guide us."

"And will you honor the land she comes from—the songs, the silence, the strength passed down from those who walked before her?" she asked gently, testing the depth of his resolve.

"I will," Lucas said without hesitation. "With all that I am."

Mama Tandiwe reached out, her weathered hand resting over his. "Then, Lucas, I have no fears. You are the answer to prayers I whispered long ago."

❧· Conversations in the Night ·❧

Later that night, Abeni and Mama Tandiwe sat by the flickering lantern inside their home. Silence filled the space between them, comfortable yet charged with unspoken words.

"Mama," Abeni said softly, breaking the silence. "What happens now? With the traditions, the expectations?"

Mama Tandiwe's lips curved into a faint smile. "Tradition carries weight, my child. The bride price must be addressed, even in your father's absence. There will be voices—voices that doubt, voices that resist. But love does not falter in the face of tradition—it finds a way to honor it."

She paused, her gaze steady. "We will call on your uncles. Though the bloodline feels fractured, the roots are still there. And even broken roots can nourish something new."

Abeni exhaled, her hands trembling slightly. "And if they refuse, Mama? If they say no because Papa isn't here?"

Mama Tandiwe took her daughter's hands into her own, her grip firm and warm. "Then we will stand, Abeni. We will stand in faith, in courage, and in love. Because this story isn't theirs to write—it's yours and Lucas'."

Abeni nodded slowly, the weight of fear softening in her chest. "Thank you for standing with me, Mama."

Mama Tandiwe's eyes glistened. "I've always stood with you. Even when the world stood against us."

The two women sat there, the glow of the lantern casting warm shadows on their faces, as the night wrapped around them like a protective embrace.

"Sometimes, shadows linger—not to haunt us, but to remind us of the light waiting just beyond their reach."

CHAPTER *Fourteen*

THREADS OF TRADITION

✑ The Gathering of Elders ✑

The village square was alive with murmurs and cautious glances as elders gathered beneath the shade of an ancient baobab tree. Wooden stools were arranged in a wide circle, their placement deliberate and symbolic. Lucas stood beside Mama Tandiwe, his expression calm but resolute. Beside him, Elder Jabari offered a reassuring nod.

The men and women representing Abeni's late father's family sat across from them, their faces stern, their eyes sharp with judgment.

Mama Tandiwe stepped forward, her shawl wrapped tightly around her shoulders, her voice steady despite the weight of the moment. "We are gathered here today to honor tradition and to seek the blessing of our ancestors on this union."

One of the elders, a tall man with a weathered face, spoke up. "Mama Tandiwe, your husband's absence left questions unanswered. There are shadows that still linger over your family. And now, you bring this foreigner before us? Is this not an insult to our customs?"

Lucas met the man's sharp gaze, his voice respectful but firm. "I understand your concerns, Elder. But my intentions are pure, and my love for Abeni is steadfast. I am here not just to ask for your blessing but to honor the traditions that have shaped her."

Another elder, an older woman with a piercing gaze, added, "Traditions are not simply words spoken in circles—they are lived, carried, and protected. Can you, Lucas, truly understand what you are stepping into?"

Lucas took a deep breath. "I may not fully understand every custom, every expectation. But I do understand love, respect, and honor. And I promise to walk this journey with Abeni, honoring her family, her roots, and the traditions she holds dear."

For a brief moment, silence stretched across the circle. Then Elder Jabari spoke, his voice carrying authority and clarity. "The measure of a man is not found in his origins, but in the integrity of his heart.

Lucas has shown his intentions through his actions, his words, and his unwavering love for Abeni."

∾· *Mama Tandiwe Speaks* ·∾

Mama Tandiwe stepped forward, her voice rising above the murmurs of the gathering. "This village knows my story. You know the accusations, the whispers. But you also know the truth that lives in the threads of every garment my daughter has stitched, in every prayer she has whispered over this village."

She turned to face the elders, her shoulders squared. "This man, Lucas, has stood beside my daughter not because of convenience or fleeting affection, but because he sees her worth. And if my husband were here today, he would see it too."

Her voice trembled slightly as she continued, "Do not let the shadows of the past rob Abeni of her future. Do not let suspicion cloud what is honest and true."

The older woman who had spoken earlier nodded slowly, her gaze softening. "Mama Tandiwe, your words carry weight. And your daughter… she carries grace."

∾· *Abeni Steps Forward* ·∾

Abeni, who had been standing quietly at the edge of the circle, stepped forward. Her dress fluttered slightly in the afternoon breeze, and her voice, though soft, carried strength.

"Elders, I have grown up honoring the ways of this village, respecting its traditions, and carrying its stories in my heart. But love… love is not bound by borders or limited by differences. Lucas has shown me kindness, respect, and a love that reflects God's own grace."

She paused, her eyes meeting each elder one by one. "I am not asking you to change tradition. I am asking you to see our hearts—to see the honesty, the sacrifice, and the commitment we bring before you today."

The silence that followed was profound, broken only by the distant hum of village life.

The Bride Price Offering

At Elder Jabari's nod, Lucas stepped forward once more. Two young boys approached, carrying baskets and bundles wrapped in kente cloth. Inside were tokens of honor: bolts of fine fabric and a symbolic payment of bride price, including a portion of the agreed number of oxen and goats, the rest to be paid in intervals as per tradition.

Lucas bowed respectfully. "With my family's blessing, I present these gifts in good faith. My parents, though unable to travel immediately, have sent letters of goodwill, and they are preparing to journey here soon to witness and honor the final celebration."

He unwrapped a folded letter, its calligraphy elegant. "My mother writes, 'Tell Abeni's family that we bless this union and we look forward to embracing our daughter with joy.'"

The Decision

Elder Jabari rose to his feet, his staff planted firmly in the ground. "The truth has been spoken here today. The weight of the past is heavy, but it does not define the present."

He turned to the other elders, his gaze firm. "This union is not a breaking of tradition—it is a bridge between two worlds, two hearts, and two families. We must not let fear guide our decisions."

After a brief but weighted pause, the eldest among them stood and spoke, his voice gravelly but clear. "We will honor this union. Let love be the thread that binds, and let tradition be the foundation on which they build."

A sigh of relief rippled through the air. Mama Tandiwe pressed a hand over her heart, tears brimming in her eyes. Abeni let out a quiet breath, her hand finding Lucas'.

Lucas nodded respectfully to the elders, his voice low and steady. "Thank you. I will honor this trust, this blessing, for as long as I live."

A Quiet Celebration

Two days later, as the sun dipped low over Nyathera, Mama Tandiwe and Abeni prepared a modest meal. Lucas helped set the table outside beneath the stars, lanterns flickering softly in the night breeze. The celebration was simple, intimate, and sacred.

Mama Tandiwe raised her cup, her voice carrying a quiet strength. "Tonight, we give thanks—to God, to love, and to the courage it takes to honor tradition while walking forward in faith."

Abeni and Lucas exchanged a glance, their hands finding each other across the table. The night wrapped them in its quiet embrace, and somewhere in the stillness, a new chapter began to unfold.

"Tradition is not a chain to hold us back, but a thread to guide us forward—a thread woven with love, courage, and faith. And in its weaving, a new legacy begins."

CHAPTER FIFTEEN

BRIDGES BETWEEN WORLDS

The sun dipped below the horizon, casting golden hues over Nyathera. The *Threads of Hope* workshop buzzed with life as young women stitched fabric, chatted quietly, and shared laughter. Lucas was helping one of the younger boys assemble wooden tables, while Abeni walked among the women, offering guidance and encouragement.

Their dream was no longer just an idea; it was alive, breathing, and changing lives.

A Letter from Home

Late one afternoon, Lucas sat on a wooden bench beneath the acacia tree, a letter trembling in his hands. It was written in his father's unmistakable handwriting.

"Lucas,

Your mother and I will be arriving in Nyathera next week. It's time we saw for ourselves what you've chosen to dedicate your life to. I won't pretend to fully understand your choices, but I owe you—and Abeni—that much.

Your father, James Sterling"

Abeni found him there moments later, her gentle presence breaking his trance.

"They're coming," Lucas said, his voice steady but his eyes filled with uncertainty.

Abeni knelt beside him, her hand covering his. "Then let them see, Lucas. Let them see the love, the purpose, and the faith that have brought us here."

∂•• The Arrival ••∂

The day the Sterlings arrived, the village seemed to hold its breath. A polished black carriage rolled into Nyathera, its refined structure a sharp contrast to the earthy simplicity of the village. Villagers paused their work, curiosity mingling with caution, as Mr. James Sterling stepped out, followed by Mrs. Eleanor Sterling, her face shaded by a wide-brimmed hat.

Lucas and Abeni stood side by side at the entrance of the *Threads of Hope* workshop. Lucas stepped forward, his voice calm and clear.

"Welcome to Nyathera, Father. Mother."

James Sterling's gaze swept over the surroundings—the modest buildings, the bustling courtyard, the villagers. His expression remained unreadable. But when Eleanor's eyes met Abeni's, her face lit up with a familiar warmth.

"Abeni," Eleanor said softly, stepping forward. Her voice carried affection and something deeper—perhaps regret, perhaps admiration. "It's so good to see you again."

Abeni smiled, her eyes bright. "Welcome back, Mrs. Sterling. It's an honor to have you here."

James cleared his throat. "Shall we see what you've built here, Lucas?"

Lucas gestured toward the workshop doors, and the group moved forward. But for a moment, Eleanor reached out and lightly squeezed Abeni's hand—a silent exchange, a bridge between two worlds.

∂•• A Walk Through the Workshop ••∂

Inside, the hum of sewing machines mingled with soft conversation and the giggles of nearby children. Shelves lined the walls, filled with neatly folded garments ready for market. Colorful quilts adorned the room like patchworks of testimony.

James paused beside a young girl sewing an intricate pattern.

"Where did she learn that?" he asked, his tone clipped but intrigued.

"Here," Abeni replied gently. "Each stitch tells a story. A story of healing, of hope."

James nodded slowly, the faintest flicker of something—perhaps respect—in his features.

Eleanor trailed behind, her fingers brushing the fabric of an embroidered tablecloth.

"It's beautiful," she whispered.

"It's built with love, ma'am. And faith," Abeni said.

Lucas added, "It's not just a workshop. It's a bridge—between struggle and purpose, between wounds and wonder."

James looked at his son, thoughtful. "You've done well here, Lucas."

❦• An Honest Conversation •❦

That evening, under the quiet shade of the acacia, Lucas and his parents sat together. Abeni remained inside with Mama Tandiwe, giving space for the moment.

James spoke first. "When you left Europe, I thought you were throwing away everything we'd built. But now... now I see you were building something greater."

Lucas nodded. "Not alone. Abeni and this village made this possible. Her vision shaped mine."

Eleanor reached over, taking Lucas' hand. "We may not have understood you then, but we do now. And we are proud of what you've become."

James exhaled slowly. "So what comes next, son? Will you stay?"

Lucas looked toward the hills beyond the village. "Yes. This is home now. And we hope... you'll stand with us when the time comes."

❧• A Moment of Grace •❧

The next morning, James found Abeni preparing tea outside her home.

"Abeni," he began, his voice quieter than usual. "I misjudged you. But now I see. You've given Lucas more than we ever could—not just purpose, but peace. For that, I thank you."

He extended a small velvet pouch. "This belonged to my grandmother. I hope you'll accept it."

Inside lay a delicate gold locket, engraved with intertwined initials.

Abeni clutched it gently, emotion catching in her throat. "Thank you, Mr. Sterling. I will treasure it."

❧• Eleanor's Visit •❧

Later that day, Eleanor returned to the workshop alone. The hum of sewing resumed around her, though eyes followed her respectfully.

She walked slowly through the space, taking in the life it carried.

"It feels... alive here," she murmured.

"It is," Abeni replied, stepping forward. "Every thread carries a prayer."

Eleanor nodded, her voice thick. "Lucas sees something eternal in you, Abeni. And now, I see it too. Don't lose that light. The world needs it."

❧• A Village United •❧

That evening, the village gathered for a quiet celebration beneath the stars. Lanterns glowed warmly, music floated through the air, and hearts swelled with something sacred.

James raised a glass. "To hope, to love, and to the courage it takes to build what lasts."

Abeni caught Eleanor's gaze across the firelight. They exchanged a smile—one of deep understanding.

As the music continued, Lucas and Abeni stood beneath the acacia tree.

"They see it now," Abeni whispered.

"They do," Lucas said, drawing her close. "And they'll carry it home with them."

"Sometimes, healing doesn't come with loud declarations, but with quiet conversations, softened hearts, and the courage to extend grace."

CHAPTER *Sixteen*

STITCHED
IN LOVE

❧• A New Day, A New Chapter •❧

Several days had passed since the elders gave their blessing. The gentle rhythm of village life resumed, but something in Nyathera had shifted—hearts were lighter, hope brighter. Lucas had returned briefly to the city to finalize paperwork and prepare his parents for their journey, while the village quietly began preparations for a sacred union.

Word had spread that the once-silent residence of the Sterlings was stirring again. A crew of local builders, working discreetly under Lucas's guidance, had been restoring the property. What was once a distant memory now emerged as a symbol of redemption.

❧• The Morning of the Wedding •❧

The sun rose gently over the hills of Nyathera, bathing the village in hues of soft lavender and gold. There was a sense of reverence in the air, woven into every thread of the preparations.

In her room, Abeni sat before the mirror. Her hair, gently woven by Mama Tandiwe's hands, was crowned with delicate white flowers. Her gown, sewn with quiet devotion by the women of the Threads of Hope workshop, flowed around her like water. Each stitch whispered the prayers of those who had walked with her.

Mama Tandiwe's voice trembled as she adjusted the neckline. "You are a vision, my daughter. Your father would have danced with joy today."

Abeni's eyes glistened. "I feel him, Mama. In every breeze. In the way the sun kisses the hills. I feel him."

❧• At the Revived Sterling Residence •❧

The morning light filtered through newly polished windows, casting a warm glow across the restored Sterling residence—now humming with quiet joy. Once worn by silence and time, the home now stood renewed, its walls graced with fresh paint and handwoven tapestries from the Threads of Hope workshop. A symbol of new beginnings and healed legacies.

Lucas stood before a mirror, adjusting the collar of his crisp white shirt with a quiet mix of anticipation and humility. The suit he wore, though tailored in a European style, bore subtle African patterns—lines and swirls reminiscent of Nyathera's heritage, stitched with reverence.

In the room with him stood two pillars of his journey—Reverend Mosi, who had traveled from a nearby town to officiate the sacred union, and Elder Jabari, whose spiritual mentorship had guided him through the rhythms of village life.

Elder Jabari moved closer, adjusting the cuffs of Lucas's sleeves with care. "Today, you step into a covenant, Lucas," he said, voice steady with paternal warmth. "Not just with Abeni, but with this village, with its people, and with the generations yet to come. Walk boldly, son."

Lucas nodded, his heart steady, his purpose clear.

Reverend Mosi offered a warm smile. "Are you ready, Lucas?"

Lucas exhaled slowly. "I've never been more ready for anything in my life."

From across the room, Eleanor and James Sterling observed quietly. The emotion on Eleanor's face shimmered in her misted eyes. Her fingers rested lightly on James's arm as they took in the space—now transformed not just by restoration, but by redemption.

James whispered, "It feels... whole again."

Eleanor nodded, watching her son prepare to begin a new chapter in a home once haunted by distance. "Because love rebuilt it."

∞· The Ceremony Beneath the Acacia Tree ·∞

The ancient acacia tree, adorned with lanterns and woven fabrics, stood as a sacred witness to a moment generations had longed to see. Beneath its sprawling branches, rows of villagers gathered in reverent silence, dressed in vibrant hues that reflected the joy of the occasion. From afar, the rhythmic beat of drums and the sweet hum of women's voices rose into the air like incense, setting a sacred atmosphere.

Lucas stood at the altar with Reverend Mosi—who had journeyed from the neighboring village of Mugumo—and Elder Jabari on either side of him. His hands were calm, but his heart thundered in gratitude and awe.

And then she came.

Abeni appeared at the end of the aisle, her arm gently tucked into that of her paternal uncle—her father's older brother, who had for years remained distant, caught in grief and silence after his brother's passing. His eyes now shimmered not only with the weight of tradition but with the healing power of reconciliation. With each step they took, a rift was mended, and the past was rewritten.

The soft strains of **"Look What the Lord Has Done"**—sung in low harmony by the village choir—filled the air. Women wept quietly as Abeni walked in grace, her veil shimmering like morning dew, her footsteps sure and sacred. Every fold of her flowing garment, stitched by the women of the Threads of Hope workshop, carried prayers of endurance, healing, and joy.

Lucas' breath caught as he beheld her. Their eyes met across the sacred space, and in that gaze, every past wound was soothed, every waiting moment redeemed.

Lucas whispered as she reached him, "You're here."

"I'm here," Abeni replied, her voice steady, her smile radiant.

The uncle stepped back, placing Abeni's hand in Lucas' with a quiet nod of approval. His voice, low and almost inaudible, carried the weight of years lost: "Take care of her. She carries more than love—she carries legacy."

Reverend Mosi cleared his throat gently and began the ceremony. "Today, we do not merely witness a wedding—we bear witness to love's triumph over time, distance, and sorrow. Lucas and Abeni, you stand beneath this tree, before your elders and your God, to declare your covenant."

Lucas turned fully toward Abeni. "You are my light, my anchor, and my greatest joy. I promise to honor you, walk with you, and build a life stitched with grace."

Abeni responded, her eyes never leaving his. "You've shown me love that is patient, and a faith that does not falter. I vow to walk beside you in strength, in peace, and in wonder."

Elder Jabari lifted their joined hands, his voice firm yet full of warmth. "What God has joined together, let no man put asunder."

Cheers erupted through the crowd as Lucas lifted Abeni's veil and kissed her gently beneath the golden light filtering through the branches. The drums picked up once more, and a new song rose—not just from the choir, but from the hearts of all who had gathered.

The Sterling Touch

As the final blessing echoed beneath the acacia tree, Eleanor Sterling stepped forward, her eyes glistening with tears. With a deep breath, she began to sing—an old hymn from her English childhood:

"Great is Thy faithfulness, O God my Father…"

The melody, once foreign to Nyathera, now wrapped itself tenderly around the village's rhythm. The women joined in with harmonies of their own, creating a transcendent blend that rose into the evening air. Even the birds seemed to pause mid-flight, as if drawn into the sacredness of the moment.

Abeni, overcome with emotion, felt her knees weaken slightly. Lucas reached for her hand and steadied her, whispering, "She's not just singing—she's welcoming you home."

As the last note faded, Eleanor stepped toward Abeni and gently placed a string of heirloom pearls into her hands. "This belonged to my grandmother," she said, her voice steady now. "I believe it's time they adorned someone who carries both legacy and promise."

Abeni was speechless. For the first time, she was not merely serving tea in a foreign home—**she was being embraced as family**.

⁓• A Celebration of Unity •⁓

The village square overflowed with joy and music. Tables were adorned with vibrant cloth, overflowing with traditional dishes—spiced plantains, stewed meats, fresh greens—and beside them, crystal trays of finger sandwiches and delicate lemon cakes from Eleanor's recipe box. It was a tapestry of cultures woven with affection.

Children twirled in circles, their laughter punctuating the beat of drums and guitars strumming side by side. No one watched the time.

Mama Tandiwe, regal in a golden headwrap and flowing indigo dress, danced slowly but joyfully with Abeni's uncle, their steps a quiet testimony of a reconciled family.

James Sterling stood on a wooden bench to address the crowd. His voice cracked as he raised his glass. "To bridges built. To wounds healed. And to a future richer than either of our families could have ever imagined on their own."

The crowd erupted in cheers and ululations, and someone began singing an old wedding chant that echoed through the hills.

⁓• A Quiet Moment by the River •⁓

As twilight fell into evening, Lucas and Abeni slipped away to the riverbank, the same place where many prayers had been whispered, and tears once shed. The moon was high, casting silver over the water's surface.

They sat on a rock worn smooth by time. Lucas pulled Abeni gently into his arms, her head resting on his chest. They said nothing for a long while.

Then Lucas whispered, "This... this is home."

"It's only the beginning," Abeni replied, her voice steady, eyes fixed on the sky.

Behind them, the faint sound of music still drifted from the celebration, but in that moment, they heard only the sound of water and destiny.

Mama Tandiwe's Blessing

Later that night, back in her quiet sewing corner, Mama Tandiwe's fingers danced along the edges of a newly started cloth—a symbol of new beginnings.

Abeni entered the room, her wedding dress still flowing, her veil draped over one shoulder like a sash of royalty.

"Mama," she said softly, emotion catching her voice.

Mama Tandiwe rose and took her daughter into her arms. "This day, my child, is proof that love—true love—can cross any sea, climb any hill, and mend even the deepest wound. Guard this love with prayer, with grace, and with the wisdom passed from those who came before you."

They held each other tightly, a legacy of faith flowing from one generation to the next.

Under the Stars

Outside their newly blessed home—now a fusion of village charm and quiet elegance—Lucas and Abeni stood side by side. The **Threads of Hope Center** glowed nearby, its lanterns softly swaying in the breeze, illuminating the vision they had sewn together from pain and promise.

Lucas looked up at the stars, then turned to her. "Are you happy, Abeni?"

She rested her head on his shoulder, her fingers laced with his. "More than I ever dreamed possible."

They stood in silence, wrapped in night, hearts stitched together—no longer from two different worlds, but from one new world they'd created in love.

> *"Some love stories are written in ink, others in whispered prayers, and a few—like this one—are stitched into the very fabric of eternity."*

EPILOGUE:

A TAPESTRY COMPLETED—BRIDGES THAT ENDURE

❧• *Sunset Over Nyathera* •❧

The sun dipped low over Nyathera, casting a warm amber glow across the village. Shadows stretched long across the cobbled paths, and the soft hum of evening life filled the air. The Threads of Hope Center stood proudly in the distance, its windows glowing softly, as though carrying the light of a thousand prayers stitched into every thread within its walls.

Under the familiar canopy of the ancient acacia tree, Abeni and Lucas sat side by side. Their children, Kairo and Ayana, played nearby—Ayana's laughter like bells in the evening air, Kairo's hands clutched tightly around a hand-carved wooden toy made by his grandfather, James Sterling.

Abeni leaned her head on Lucas' shoulder, her voice soft but steady. "Do you ever stop to wonder, Lucas… how every moment led us here? Every choice, every prayer, every tear—it all stitched us into this moment."

Lucas smiled, pressing a gentle kiss to her hair. "I think about it every day, Abeni. And I still marvel at how one letter from your hands turned into a life woven with grace."

❧• *The Threads of Hope Legacy* •❧

The Threads of Hope Center had grown over the years—not just in size, but in spirit. Young women traveled from distant villages to learn the craft of sewing, but they left with so much more than a skill. They carried confidence, dignity, and the knowledge that their stories mattered.

Lucas had helped establish trade connections with distant markets, bringing Nyathera's vibrant fabrics to faraway cities. Each garment carried not just patterns and stitches, but prayers whispered over every thread.

Eleanor Sterling, now affectionately called Gogo Eléa by the village children, taught English and storytelling classes under the shaded veranda. What began as a visit had grown into a life purpose, her once-reserved heart now deeply entwined with the rhythms of Nyathera.

James, too, found quiet joy in woodworking, often crafting toys for the children or benches for the Center's courtyard.

Mama Tandiwe had grown older, her hair now silver like moonlight, but her hands were still steady as she worked the needle. She often sat in the courtyard of the workshop, surrounded by the laughter of women and children, her heart full of gratitude.

Abeni walked through the workshop often, her presence a quiet force of grace and wisdom. She spoke softly to the young women, guiding their hands as they worked, offering words of encouragement when seams unraveled.

"Every stitch is a prayer," she would remind them. "Every thread carries a story."

∽• Reflections by the River •∽

One quiet evening, Abeni and Lucas took a familiar walk to the riverbank. The water glistened under the moonlight, its surface reflecting the starlit sky.

"This place..." Lucas began, his voice thick with emotion. "It feels like everything began here, Abeni. Every promise, every dream—it was all whispered into these waters."

Abeni smiled, her hand resting over the pendant around her neck—the same pendant Lucas had once given her all those years ago. Its surface was worn now, but it still caught the moonlight just as it had on the night of his proposal.

"God brought us here, Lucas. Through every storm, every doubt, every whisper of fear... He carried us," Abeni said softly.

Lucas nodded, his gaze fixed on the water. "And He will continue to carry us, Abeni. Every day, every season."

Their fingers intertwined, their silhouettes framed against the shimmering river—a portrait of love that had weathered storms and bloomed in grace.

❧ A Letter to the Future ·❧

Years later, on a quiet afternoon, Abeni sat at her sewing table, a sheet of parchment before her. She dipped her quill into ink and began to write.

"To the dreamers, the builders, the ones who dare to hope…"

"This workshop, these threads, and these stories—they are not just ours. They belong to every hand that has stitched, every voice that has sung, and every prayer that has been whispered within these walls."

"May you always remember that love is not just spoken—it is stitched into the fabric of our lives. Faith is not just felt—it is the thread that binds every broken piece together. And hope… hope is the light that keeps us moving forward, even when the path seems unclear."

"Carry this legacy with care. Protect it, nurture it, and let it grow. For every thread matters. Every story matters. And every heart, no matter how fragile, can be stitched whole again."

—With love, Abeni Sterling

She folded the letter carefully and placed it inside a small wooden box, where it joined other keepsakes—a dried flower from their wedding day, a swatch of the first quilt stitched at the workshop, and the pendant Lucas had once given her.

❧ The Acacia Tree at Dusk ·❧

The sun dipped below the horizon, and lanterns began to flicker across the village square. Under the acacia tree, Abeni and Lucas stood together, their children running circles around them, their laughter mingling with the gentle rustle of the wind.

The Threads of Hope Center glowed softly in the distance, a beacon of love and resilience.

"Abeni," Lucas said softly, his arm wrapped around her shoulders. "Do you think they'll remember us? Long after we're gone?"

Abeni smiled, her gaze distant but warm. "Not just us, Lucas. They'll remember the stories, the prayers, the love stitched into every corner of this village. And the bridges we built—between worlds, between wounds, between generations. And that... that is enough."

As night settled over Nyathera, the stars emerged one by one, scattered like diamonds across an endless canvas. The wind carried faint whispers through the leaves of the acacia tree—a tree that had witnessed love, loss, promises, and renewal.

"Every thread tells a story. Every stitch carries a promise. And when woven with love, faith, and hope, even the most fragile fibers become a tapestry strong enough to bridge worlds, heal hearts, and leave a legacy that endures."

"In every sunrise, in every whispered prayer, and in every quiet moment under the acacia tree, love remains—the thread that binds us all."

"Some love stories are written on pages, others are whispered in prayers, but the most enduring ones are stitched into the very fabric of eternity."

The End

ABOUT THE AUTHOR

ynthia Chirinda is a Transformation Catalyst, Systems Change Practitioner, and Personal Development Coach committed to helping individuals and institutions thrive in purpose-driven alignment. Her work bridges faith, leadership, healing, and nation-building—reaching across boardrooms, grassroots communities, and policy arenas.

Cynthia is the Founder of Wholeness Incorporated, a visionary consultancy that provokes critical thinking and champions restorative approaches to personal, organizational, and societal transformation. She is also the Director of Africa Reform Institute, empowering citizens to engage in values-based leadership for sustainable development, and the founder of WOPIZ – Women Politicians' Incubator Zimbabwe, an initiative committed to mentoring and equipping women for political and public leadership.

With a strong Pan-African worldview and a passion for authentic development, Cynthia has worked extensively in strategy design, team and leadership development, research, communication, and institutional transformation—leveraging over a decade of experience in designing solutions that endure.

Cynthia is a prolific author, coach, and public speaker, whose messages ignite reflection, activate purpose, and cultivate wholeness. Her training expertise spans areas including:

- Transformational Leadership & Strategy Design
- Communication & Executive Presence
- Vitality, Wellness & Balanced Living
- Team Development & Coaching
- Women's Empowerment & Nation Building
- Christian Leadership & Spiritual Exhortation

She is the author of numerous life-shaping books, including:
- *The Connection Factor Series* (Personal Growth, Women, Leaders)
- *Can the Whole Woman Please Stand Up!*
- *Managing Transitions: Navigating Change with Grace*
- *The Whole You – Vital Keys for Balanced Living*
- *Destination Wholeness – Going Beyond Brokenness*
- *You Are Not Damaged Goods* series (*Reboot and Start Afresh, Blossom and Flourish, Transitioning from Tragedies to Triumph*)
- *The Wealthy Diary of African Wisdom*
- *Intelligent Conversations – A Mindset Shift Towards a Developed Africa*
- *Whole Enough to Go: Embracing God's Call in Imperfection*

Co-authored works:
- *Success Within Reach*
- *Reinvented and Victorious: The Anthology*

She is also the visionary behind:
- *Intelligent Conversations with Cynthia:* A broadcast program promoting transformative dialogue on leadership and societal development globally.
- *Women Rising in Africa (WORIA):* A program profiling women across Africa who rise against odds to empower their communities and nations.
- *The Extra Mile* – A documentary film celebrating women leading in positive nation-building initiatives. Cynthia believes that wholeness is not about achieving perfection but courageously embracing life's transitions with faith and resilience. Her work continues to inspire individuals globally, offering hope, clarity, and the tools to live purpose-driven lives.

Cynthia believes that wholeness is not about perfection—it is about intentionality, truth, and a deep surrender to God's purpose in every season of life. She continues to use her platforms to incubate transformational leaders, elevate strategic solutions, and co-create the Africa we all want to live in.

Connect with Cynthia:
Website: www.cynthiachirinda.com
Email: info@cynthiachirinda.com
LinkedIn: Cynthia Chirinda

www.ingramcontent.com/pod-product-compliance
Lightning Source LLC
Chambersburg PA
CBHW050350030726
47503CB00008B/2703